A Boy's Life
with Older Sisters

STANLEY B. TRICE

Copyright © 2022 by Stanley B. Trice
Published by Every Word Rise, LLC
Place of Publication: New Bern, NC

Cover and formatting by Woven Red Author Services, www.WovenRed.ca

Library of Congress Control Number: 2022910880

ISBN for Print:978-0-9909265-7-3
ISBN for Ebook:978-0-9909265-8-0

Other Books by
Stanley B. Trice

High School Rocket Science (For Extraterrestrial Use Only)

Evidence of a Commuter Train

A Chance to Tell Ten Stories

Contents

Dennis is Finally Ten Years Old

Soon after turning ten-years-old, Dennis started paying more attention to what was going on around him. He figured it was about time since he was now part of the double-digit age. He felt so much more mature with two numbers to his age, rather than one.

The first thing he paid more attention to was his morning bus ride. The school was fourteen miles away, yet it took the bus an hour to get there. It picked up Dennis first, then circled the school three times, picking up other kids before pulling into the narrow school parking lot. There was no reason to have a bigger parking lot since no one at the school was old enough to drive, except the teachers and staff.

In the morning, Dennis had his pick of any seat. Yet, he always sat exactly in the same place. It was the sixth seat from the front, on the driver's side, and against the window. That left six seats separating him from the back of the bus.

Dennis favored even numbers, window views, and the middle of things. Sitting there, he imagined he was riding in a rocket ship with a portal from where he watched planets (buildings) and other spaceships (vehicles) passing by. Also, for most of the ride he had the seat to himself since kids sat in the front to see where they were going or in the back because they didn't care.

Front and back seat kids sometimes teased Dennis that the middle of the bus was so middle-of-the-bus, as if the front and back seats were special. Dennis thought about how all the seats were the same. Some just had a different view than others, and he enjoyed his views. Besides, they all got to the school together at the same time.

When the front and back seats filled up, someone eventually had to sit next to Dennis. On a crowded bus picking up from multiple neighborhoods, it was always a different kid. Before reaching the school, Dennis started a conversation that generally went like this:

"I'm Dennis. What's your name?"

The student, unprepared for an introduction, said their first name.

"What's your last name?"

Still unprepared, as most middle schoolers, the kid usually said a last name and waited to answer more questions or dared Dennis not to bother them again.

"My last name is Smith. This bus could be a yellow spaceship taking us to another galaxy," Dennis said.

This is the part where middle schooler either ignored Dennis, made a comment that included "stupid," or asked, "What video game is that?"

Dennis explained how video games made him dizzy. The middle schooler usually laughed at Dennis before saying "stupid" a few times, hoping to ward off whatever Dennis had. Video games were important to many kids, like an addiction, Dennis had concluded.

Without the kid knowing, Dennis wrote their name in a notebook, in case the middle schooler became famous one day. That way he had proof that he met the famous person and maybe he could use their name to meet them again after they were famous. Dennis hoped the student was famous in a good way. He didn't want to be profiled on some future TV crime show for knowing someone famous enough to be on a TV crime show.

Dennis's bus dumped him at school in time to run for homeroom, starting his stress off. He disliked being late and suspected the bus driver knew this. She always had a wicked smile as he stumbled down the bus stairs.

At school, Dennis sat in the middle of the classroom so no one would notice him. He saw how teachers paid attention to those in the front who wanted the attention and to the students in the back who did not want it, but got attention anyway for being in the back. The middle became a safe place for someone like him.

When front and back seats were filled, the kids who were forced to sit in the middle of the classroom with Dennis were of three types. Those who complained about missing out on the front row seats, although they pretended they were in the front, anyway. There were also kids who wanted to be in the back row and who scooted their desks in that direction. The rest wanted to be outside, away from books and kids like Dennis, who preferred to be in the middle of the classroom.

To Dennis, the middle of the classroom was a safe place to keep from talking to kids he didn't understand that much.

At lunch, he ate slower than others and had no time to debate the loudness of someone's fart. After school, boys he barely talked to demanded he do things with them he wasn't interested in doing when he was alone.

After an hour bus ride in the afternoon and being the last one dropped off, Dennis always gave the driver a smile. A different driver than the morning bus, she gave him a look that she wanted him off the bus so she could go home. She had no smile with this look. Dennis hoped she found her smile at home.

Before homework or a snack and before his three older sisters noticed he was home, Dennis escaped on his bike. He rode the one-mile-long cul-de-sac five times back and forth, pretending he was traveling through outer space in a flying saucer. The suburban, ranch-style houses he passed over and over became alien planets where extraterrestrials lived.

Inside these houses, he imagined strange life forms existing who were just too weird to live anywhere else but in those mysterious houses. Beings who could be as weird as his sisters with their alien personalities.

His Sisters

Twelve-year-old Wendy had red hair from some ancient ancestry that none of them shared. When she flipped her hair around, it was as if her redness was a sword challenging anyone who looked her way. That included her brother.

Fourteen-year-old Glenda hated equally her thick brown hair that seemed to strangle her face and her pale body that stored the food she loved. She complained to Dennis about many things, none of which Dennis understood. He figured Glenda would be the first with a tattoo. He tried to avoid her.

Sixteen-year-old Sarah had the darkest complexion, longest black hair, and strived to be the thinnest and tallest family member. Her fierce stare was her best look. She scared Dennis.

In contrast to his sisters, Dennis had wavy brown hair, brown eyes, and a slight brown look that made him think about brown too much. Somehow, the red freckles on his round face could still be seen, despite all the brownness.

All four of them went to schools clustered on both sides of a two-lane road. Wendy's junior high sat across the road from the senior high school that Glenda and Sarah attended. The middle school Dennis went to was on the other side of the wide, senior high parking lot.

The schools were a short walk from each other, yet his sisters had cultivated separate rides from their separate friends, leaving Dennis to ride the bus since he had no friends. One day he hoped to understand his sisters' culture that left their brother unincluded and vulnerable to long bus rides.

At least the bus ride gave him more time to read his science fiction books. Some from the library and some from used book stores. Reading books online made his eyes jiggle, squint, and otherwise make him go back to real books.

Dennis read about ghosts, extraterrestrials, and unknown undiscovered beings on other worlds, all of whom reminded him of his sisters.

He believed they had to have come from another planet. They were always yelling at each other about their feelings he did not understand. They even had opinions about their feelings and disagreements among themselves, even if they shared the same opinions and feelings. It confused Dennis.

When they got bored yelling at each other, they had opinions and feelings about him. This criticism included what he wore, how he looked, and that he was too quiet. Dennis liked his life style despite their feelings, opinions, and criticism. His parents were of no help.

Mother's brown eyes, short dark curly hair, and dark complexion were misunderstood by people thinking she had African ancestry. No, she explained, Sicily was not a part of Africa. Dennis planned to have a DNA test when he got old enough.

Papa had gray eyes that went with his personality. He might have had blond hair, but he didn't have much of it anymore. He was happy reading the online news from Sweden and Ireland, although his ancestors came from Spain and Scotland.

Mother was taller than Papa by two inches and she enjoyed wearing high heels to be even taller. Papa didn't mind since it attracted attention toward his wife and away from him. He liked mingling in the shadows, he would say. Both his parents seemed comfortable in their roles of varying heights. This comfortableness extended to them working together.

They were into numbers, yet in different ways. Papa was the third partner in an accounting firm managing local business accounts. The firm's name, Hugh Hugh, sounded to Dennis like an owl's hoo hoo.

Papa's key role was keeping the clients happy when their numbers dipped toward minuses. Mother worked part time as the firm's bookkeeper and was glad she did not have to deal with clients or be full time. She would often say how she needed time for herself and away from the annoying people who came to a place called Hugh Hugh.

Dennis wasn't sure what Mother was doing with her extra time. They lived just outside a small city that was big enough not to be called a town. There was one sprawling outdoor mall area with a cluster of smaller strip malls scattered elsewhere in places that mostly didn't need one there.

Many people commuted north to the bigger city that had more money and people talked a lot. Dennis was glad his parents didn't want to live there. There were way too many people talking all the time. Their debating and opinions they said to each other seemed disconnected from reality. The people sounded like they were in a video game.

Those who did not commute north found work in the smaller city, catering to the people who commuted. Dennis enjoyed living in what the commuters called a bedroom community. It sounded cozy and happy.

The Home

Their house had two floors. An upstairs with bedrooms and bathrooms and the downstairs with the rest of the rooms. A wide back porch made up for the narrow front porch. Dennis thought of the upstairs as a place to sleep or be alone and the downstairs where people talked and ate. Most of the time, his sisters occupied the downstairs and he the upstairs. This defined their relationship at the time.

In late fall when the leaves had fallen, collected by Papa, and fallen again, Dennis saw the single oak tree in their backyard as a refuge. A place he could build a treehouse and get away from his sisters.

The oak tree was a survivor of human habitation since George Washington was President. Its trunk went up ten feet to where the wide limbs branched out in an enormous crown. The builders of any house probably thought it easier to build elsewhere than to take down the massive tree.

At the point where the heavy branches struck out from the wide trunk and toward the sky, they created a broad dip where Dennis could sit and forget he had sisters. Papa understood.

He helped his son tie boards onto the thick limbs to create walls, in case Dennis went to sleep and fell through. Papa bought a heavy piece of rope that Dennis tied into a ladder, like macrame.

He could pull it up and escape into the arms of the thick branches and be free to live in his own world.

In his tree house, Dennis felt safe from feelings, opinions, arguments, and yelling. He could read his science fiction books without interruption.

The first afternoon he was up in his tree house, Glenda stood at the base of the tree.

"I want to come up," she yelled.

"There's not enough room." Dennis lied.

"At least drop the rope ladder down so I can climb up and see."

"I'm trying to read," Dennis yelled down.

"I'll come up when you're not there and I won't let you up," Glenda said.

"Fine, I'll let you come up to see just this once." Dennis hoped his sister could tell by his voice that he was disappointed.

"Never mind. You sound disappointed. I was just seeing if you would. That tree house is your space," said Glenda, going back into the house.

He did not see the point of having sisters. At least he knew the other two wouldn't try coming up to his tree house. They probably wanted him to live in their so they could fight over who would have his room.

Being alone in the arms of the massive tree gave Dennis time to think about being a member of the double-digit age. At ten-years-old, he grew thoughts and stumbled into decisions that helped him understand a little more about himself. Then, Grandpapa came to visit.

Where Grandpapa Fits In

Soon after the creation of the tree house and on a Saturday morning in early fall, Grandpapa stood naked in the upstairs hallway. At least that much ten-year-old Dennis understood when his three older sisters came screaming down the carpeted stairs.

He was downstairs, looking out the kitchen window toward the street. Ten minutes before, Grandmother had shoved her husband into the foyer and left him standing there like an unwanted package. This caused Dennis's mother, who had opened the door, to sling a cloud of swear words toward her mother to take her father back.

For an older woman, Grandmother was pretty agile and got in her car before Mother could catch her. But Mother took track in high school and she ran in the street, preventing Grandmother from driving away. Watching the action from the window, Dennis figured Grandmother didn't want to mess up her new two-door sedan by running over her daughter.

While Mother stood in the street yelling at her mother and drawing out the neighbors, the sisters exploded out into the lawn screaming about naked Grandpapa. Mother came back only because Grandmother took the sudden diversion to drive around her daughter and escape.

Back in the house, the sisters' screaming gradually subsided into an incoherent babble. Papa asked his wife, "Why did your mother bring your father here?"

"I don't know why she dumped him on me. So what if he rubs his crotch in front of her canasta partners? She married him."

"Isn't your father dying?" Papa asked.

"Yeah, his kidneys are failing and giving him dementia or delirium. I don't know which. That's why she needs to take him back. I don't want my father dying here. I'm going after her. You get the kids to take care of whatever my father is doing upstairs."

Dennis thought their house would be a good place for Grandpapa to die in. It would drive his sisters crazy. With Grandpapa still naked upstairs, Papa wasted no time in handing out duties for the upkeep of the elder.

Knowing the stubbornness of his wife and mother-in-law, Papa made upkeep plans for the next couple of weeks. Being the only son and youngest child, Dennis figured he wouldn't be assigned anything difficult.

"Dennis, go upstairs and take your Grandpapa to the toilet. Then, help him get dressed," Papa said loud enough to be heard over his still babbling daughters.

Dennis didn't understand how the only male heir got designated as toilet boy. "That's something the sisters should do. They're older than me."

Papa looked at his daughters. They erupted into a banshee-like howl about seeing naked Grandpapa that left Papa and Dennis looking at each other as if questioning whether they were all related.

"All you need to do is tell him where to go and what to do. He isn't that far gone," said Papa.

Dennis agreed, only to escape the shrieking of his sisters. He wondered why Papa wasn't the one taking care of the elder man upstairs. Looking at his sisters in full drama mode, Dennis figured Grandpapa would be easier to deal with than his emotional sisters.

Dennis questioned the "far gone" since the elder was still standing naked in the upstairs hallway, scratching his crotch. If I was still in the single digit age, Papa would probably have been here instead of me, Dennis thought. Being ten years old was not starting off so well.

Avoiding all that scratching and nakedness, Dennis gathered up his clothes and pointed the elder towards the hallway bathroom he shuffled into. Grandpapa sat on the toilet with a grunt.

Dennis stood in the doorway, figuring his grandpapa had finished when he stood up. Not wanting to see an old man's poop and pee, Dennis kept his eyes closed while flushing the toilet. He handed Grandpapa's clothes to put back on.

Fully clothed, Dennis brought him into the hallway, where he messed in his pants, front and back. Dennis called his sisters, since his job was taking Grandpapa to the toilet and getting him dressed. By the time they found out that Grandpapa had messed in his pants, he was standing in their bedroom looking for a place to sit.

Dennis hid in his treehouse until the screaming stopped and Mother came home, unsuccessful at getting rid of her father.

The next morning on Sunday, Papa assigned Dennis to take Grandpapa to the toilet to make sure things came out in the toilet and not somewhere else. Dennis figured it was punishment from the previous evening, but it had been worth tormenting his sisters.

Dennis went upstairs and motioned with his hands for Grandpapa to sit up and down again and again over the toilet. Dennis felt like an orchestra leader. In the middle of this up and down, the old man pooped and peed everywhere but in the toilet.

Dennis was to keep Grandpapa clean, which he did. He delivered his unsoiled and fully dressed Grandpapa to his sisters, not telling them he used their bathroom and not the generic one in the hallway that was also his bathroom.

Dennis spent a few hours in his treehouse hiding from his sisters' screaming when they went to use their bathroom to get ready for church. He thought his sisters were screaming a lot since Grandpapa arrived.

In the treehouse on his smartphone, Dennis downloaded a library book about the stages of death. He could not figure out what stage of death Grandpapa was in. The elder did not look like the pictures, but Dennis also never looked at his grandpapa as a person dying.

Maybe he was already dead, like a zombie, Dennis thought. He downloaded a book about zombies. They looked more like his sisters without their makeup.

That evening after supper, Dennis approached Papa as he was going to bed.

"Why isn't Grandpapa in hospice?" Dennis's question caused his father to frown.

"Your mother and grandmother are afraid he'll tell strangers stuff they don't want anyone knowing," Papa said.

"Like what?"

"Just stuff." Papa continued to his bedroom.

Dennis considered asking his mother, but she sat in the living room watching some reality show about a bachelorette or a bachelor. It was hard to tell since everyone looked alike. Dennis figured this was her escape from having a demented and dying father in her house.

His sisters were in their room, probably playing on their social media to escape the reality of a confused Grandpapa in the guest bedroom. Dennis looked in on his grandpapa.

He found him sleeping on his back, looking dead, but breathing. Dennis checked. He wondered if Grandpapa was practicing at being dead.

The next morning before Dennis went to school, Papa explained to the family that he had a talk with his father-in-law. Turns out, the elder knew how to use the toilet. He was confused as to which rooms were which.

Dennis left to catch the bus as Papa took his father-in-law on a tour of the house. When Dennis got home, Papa had taped a sign on the door of each room explaining what was inside.

Over the sisters' doorway, Papa hung a skull and crossbones sign. Dennis considered getting a skull and crossbones for his door, too. His sign was just labeled "Dennis Room," like it was an invitation to enter.

Papa labeled the upstairs hallway bathroom "Toilet" in large letters and underlined. It wasn't labeled "Bathroom" because Grandpapa didn't like taking baths, obvious from his body odor. He took showers when Papa convinced his father-in-law that the shower water was not someone pissing on him.

After his bike ride that afternoon, Dennis found his grandpapa standing in the upstairs hallway reading the signs.

"What are you looking for, Grandpapa?"

The elderly man leaned against the wall and pointed at his crotch.

"The older I got, the smaller it got," Grandpapa said, while letting out a loud fart. "I don't remember the last time it stood at attention. I was wondering if I could find a cure in one of these rooms."

Dennis told him it was nap time and led him to bed. After supper, Dennis brought Grandpapa his supper on a tray because Mother wouldn't allow him at the kitchen table with the family. Dennis watched him eat the food carefully, as if it was his last meal. One day it would be, he thought.

Bringing the tray back to the kitchen, Dennis sat at the table across from Papa, who was reading the morning's printed newspaper. Dennis was glad printed newspapers still existed for his papa to read them alone, letting him escape from his day's experiences.

"Why doesn't my mother spend time with her father?" Dennis asked as Papa turned a page.

The drone of female chatter bled from the other rooms. Dennis didn't care what his sisters and mother were talking about, and Papa obviously didn't either.

"Sometimes people just don't like each other." He continued reading that morning's newspaper.

"Isn't anyone worried Grandpapa will die soon?" Dennis wondered if Papa was reading the comics. It was the only relevant news twelve hours later.

"As far as everyone is concerned, it won't be soon enough."

"Why doesn't my mother talk to her papa?"

"Why don't you go read your book and forget what's going on between your mother and her father?"

Dennis didn't know how he could forget. The tension in the house was already high with the daily dramas between his sisters and Grandpapa. Between Mother and her father, the tension was worse.

Papa held the newspaper up to his face, making it hard for Dennis to ask him any more questions. Dennis pulled out his smartphone and played a video game that made chirping sounds and didn't flash too much to make him dizzy. Papa left to read his newspaper in his bedroom muttering about the annoying chirping.

At bedtime, the sisters confronted Dennis in the hallway.

"Don't push the subject about Mom and Grandpapa," they all said at once. They may have talked separately, but Dennis found it hard to tell when they all sounded the same.

"Everyone seems to know some family secret about him except me," he said.

"Just shut up. You're too young to know what this is all about," said Glenda.

"I'm old enough to know there's some secret with Grandpapa that everyone knows about except me," Dennis said.

"Just accept that you're not old enough," said Wendy, who was only two years older.

"We'll tell you when we think you're old enough and ready," said Sarah, who led the others to their bedroom.

Dennis resented his sisters deciding when he was old enough for anything. He vowed to find out the secret and keep it a secret that he knew. He was excited. It would be the first secret he ever kept.

On Saturday, Papa went to work and Dennis found himself alone with a house full of women whispering about Grandpapa. Dennis tried to convince himself he wasn't interested in their talk and after lunch he took Grandpapa his tray of food.

The elderly man sat in his fake leather recliner as Dennis put the tray in his lap. As he did so, the elder announced, "I love you, darling."

"I'm not Grandmother," Dennis said. He wondered if he was looking like a girl. Living with females can be dangerous that way, he thought.

Along with the bed and chair was a brown dresser on top of which sat a TV. Before Dennis turned it on, he heard his mother downstairs talking loudly on her smartphone to Grandmother.

"I want you to take him back. You can put him away in a home somewhere. I don't care where," yelled Mother.

Dennis went into the hallway and peered over the banisters. His sisters stood in the living room doorway, facing Mother who stood in the foyer. Her high-pitched voice could be heard anywhere in the house. No matter where anyone stood.

"I do see a point in arguing about this. I don't want him here anymore. You take him back and put in hospice. I don't care what he tells people." Mother's tense voice suffered through the house.

After a brief pause, she said, "No, I don't want him here in hospice, either." A longer pause until Mother said, "He may be my father, but he's your husband and you chose him." Mother ended the call and stomped her feet into the kitchen. Dennis worried they would not be getting any Christmas presents from that side of the family.

He went back and found Grandpapa slumped over in the chair in some wilted fashion, obviously hearing everything. Dennis switched on the TV and turned the volume up so Grandpapa wouldn't hear anything more from his daughter.

In the morning while everyone got ready for church, Dennis found Grandpapa sitting on the edge of his bed in his underwear. He told Dennis, "Men don't need women as sex partners. Men can have sex partners with other men."

Dennis did not want to talk about this on church day. He was already in trouble with church beliefs after believing in extraterrestrials. Thinking about it, he didn't want to talk about sex with Grandpapa on any day.

"I don't want to hear about sex. I know about it already," Dennis answered.

With parental controls still on for his use of TV and internet, what Dennis knew about sex was what he overheard in middle school. But he didn't want to hear the details from Grandpapa.

"Before I got ill, your mother saw me kissing a man. I didn't mean for her to find out that way," Grandpapa said.

Dennis wondered what kind of kiss. Like a peck or something long and drawn out? Knowing Grandpapa kissed someone other than Grandmother sounded like cheating, whether it was a man or a woman.

He helped Grandpapa put on a shirt and pants and take him downstairs to the living room. There, the elder sat on the sofa watching a cooking show Dennis turned on before they all left for church. Dennis wondered if Grandpapa knew how to cook and if he got hungry watching cooking shows.

That evening, he led Grandpapa to the guest bedroom and brought him his supper. Mother still did not allow him to sit with them at the table as a family, even on church day. Dennis turned the TV on to travel shows.

Later, he went to help Grandpapa get ready for bed. After shedding his clothes down to his underwear, the elder climbed under the covers. As Dennis pulled the blanket over him, his grandpapa swiftly grabbed his grandson's arm.

Either Grandpapa was stronger than he looked or Dennis was weaker than he thought. He struggled to pry Grandpapa's fingers off while the elder talked about men and sex.

Even though he didn't go into the details, Dennis tried not to listen. He knew generally about gay men and women and thought it natural for two people of the same sex to like each other. After all, they were the same sex and should understand each other's body needs better than the opposite sex. This was something else the church and he disagreed on.

But he wasn't ready to hear about positions and pleasure points. He finally broke free, covered Grandpapa, and went looking for Papa.

He was in the kitchen reading the morning newspaper again. Dennis asked, "Why do men like men and not women? And the same for women, now that I'm thinking of it. Also, why do some people think this is wrong?"

Outside the kitchen window, rain fell in spurts. First drenching, then pitter-patter, then drenching. The look on Papa's face was like Dennis had pushed him into the rain when it was drenching.

"Why do you ask?"

"I think Grandpapa likes men and not women."

"Do you like boys?"

Dennis didn't like boys, girls, or his sisters. "I don't like anyone."

"Good. Keep it that way. You don't need to be in a relationship, whether it's with males or females. But in the future if you grow up to like men, that's okay with me. It'll probably be all right with your mother and sisters, but they may have an opinion about it."

Papa went back to his newspaper. Dennis stayed there at the kitchen table, watching the rain. He could smell the old cooking smells of the kitchen grow between them. Upstairs, the sisters screeched and Mother denounced Grandpapa's naked existence in the hallway. Papa left to referee the latest drama. Apparently, Grandpapa was holding the skull and crossbones sign off the sisters' door in front of his crotch. Dennis giggled and read Papa's comics.

Over the next few weeks, Mother allowed a hospice nurse to come several times a week to see if her father was still alive. Meanwhile, the sisters' behavior had gone from dramatic to melodramatic, and Papa was getting a headache each evening. Papa asked his son to help more with Grandpapa.

Knowing his grandson was taking care of him made Grandpapa not act up so much. The two fell into a routine where, after his bike ride, Dennis made sure Grandpapa was not in his sisters' room, had been to the toilet, had made his business in the toilet and nowhere else, and had all his clothes on. He wandered around the house annoying his sisters, which Dennis encouraged.

After supper, Dennis brought him his tray of food and left the elder watching travel shows on TV. Later, Dennis came to get the tray and make sure Grandpapa was in his bed and not someone else's. As part of their routine, Dennis sat in the recliner with a spiral notebook and wrote the secrets Grandpapa spoke about before going to sleep.

The stories explored Mother's childhood. They included Grandmother's ancestry in addition to Grandpapa's side of the family. Turns out, liking the same sex ran in the family, both sides. Dennis told no one, not even Papa. Each evening as Grandpapa's memory dump helped him drift off to sleep, Dennis filled several spiral notebooks.

One Thursday evening after supper, Papa took his daughters to the high school. Sarah was playing on the basketball team and the other two wanted to meet their girlfriends for gossip time. Dennis left Grandpapa with his tray of food and found his mother in the kitchen.

He couldn't remember the last time it was just the two of them alone. He wasn't sure what to say among the leftover supper smells as his mother stood at the sink cleaning dishes with an empty and working dishwasher nearby.

He remembered earlier that afternoon when Mother and Grandpapa yelled at each other. They were both in the living room, and Dennis didn't wait around to hear what it was about. He followed his sisters and Papa to places in and outside the house where the words could not reach. Based on her scrubbing, Dennis suspected Mother had issues with either the dishes or the words from earlier.

"What do you want?" Her monotone voice erupted from the area of suds and water.

"Did you ever see Grandpapa kiss a man?"

Mother's sudden stillness echoed through the kitchen and into the universe. Somewhere a star probably went nova from the silence. As Dennis stared at his mother's back and his mother stared into the sudsy sink, Grandpapa wandered in.

"Go back to your room," Dennis whispered to him. Dennis felt it couldn't go well with his mother after he asked *the question*. Besides, he did not want to talk about Grandpapa while he was there.

"You never told anyone you saw me," Grandpapa said to Mother.

"I didn't want anyone to know. I pretended it didn't happen. How did Mom find out?" Her voice sounded like she didn't want to know the answer. Mother crashed dishes into the sink. Some broke.

"I told her. I wanted her to know before my end came."

"I don't want to know you anymore." Mother had run out of dishes to crash.

"Wasn't I a good father?"

"That has nothing to do with it."

"I gave up a lot to stay with you and your mother. I could have been somebody else."

"Why did you have to say anything? Why didn't you keep it a secret? I kept it a secret. Why does everyone need to know everything about you?"

"I want people to know who I am. I don't want my secrets to die with me. I want my family to remember me not for keeping secrets, but for being who I really was."

"What makes me mad is, after all these years, you cheated on Mom. I wish you were not my father." Mother turned to face her father.

She gave Dennis a look that told him to leave quickly. Dennis took the clue and went to his room. He never asked his mother what happened after he left. But Grandpapa stopped telling family secrets to Dennis.

Two days later on Halloween afternoon, Sarah was passing Grandpapa's room when she smelled something. Normally she yelled for Dennis or Papa to check it out, yet this smell was different. She peeked inside the room.

Dennis was bringing his grandpapa the dinner tray and was three steps from the room when Sarah screamed.

Wendy and Glenda ran past Dennis and joined Sarah in a chorus of screaming as Dennis put down the tray and ran in. Grandpapa was on his back in bed, looking as if he was asleep. Of course, no one could sleep through all that screaming unless they were dead.

As the sisters flew downstairs into the living room and away from seeing a dead person for the first time, Mother appeared in her father's doorway. She spit at him lying in his bed. She did not have enough juice in her spit and it landed on the floor.

Dennis thought the spitting was some cultural thing from her side of the family. Mother left with an angry grimace that made Dennis think he could be wrong.

Before realizing he was alone with a dead person, Papa came in, avoided the spit, and stared at Grandpapa's sunken face. Grandpapa was still not breathing.

As Papa made phone calls on his smartphone, the first trick-or-treaters rang the doorbell.

Eventually, the ambulance, a fire truck, police, and finally the hospice nurse came to verify that, yes, Grandpapa was dead from natural causes. Each time someone showed up, they had to scoot around trick-or-treaters who wanted to join the costume party upstairs.

Mother handed out candy, pretending nothing was wrong while trying to comfort her daughters. Dennis stayed in the kitchen as Papa directed the professionals where to find his dead father-in-law.

As each authority announced death, Dennis's sisters wailed away in the living room and the doorbell rang for more candy. One trick-or-treater looked like dead Grandpapa, except for the hatchet buried in the head. Word got out that someone actually died upstairs and soon a crowd gathered on the lawn.

The crowd parted to let two funeral workers wheel a metal stretcher out of the house. On top was a black plastic bag covering something unmoving. Memories cemented in everyone's minds that Halloween night. Dennis watched Grandpapa's lifeless body be wheeled away among people dressed like the dead.

After the hearse left in a puff of blue smoke, Dennis went to Grandpapa's bedroom where the bed covers laid on the carpeted floor. All that was left on the bed was Grandpapa's pillow he died on. It had a slight dimple from the impression of his head.

Dennis stood there in his Dracula outfit, realizing he had missed Halloween. He started to leave and change clothes when he smelled something lurking in the bedroom. Like a vanilla smell.

He sniffed again and wondered if this was what death smelled like. Something that was good in coffee and cupcakes.

Mother called the sisters into the kitchen and they all looked at Dennis when he came to join them. He had changed clothes, which didn't help him from getting the look of go-away. Papa came in and motioned for his son to go somewhere else. Dennis concluded Mother was now in charge of her father, since he was dead.

It was too dark to climb into his treehouse, so Dennis went to the living room that had the best TV and watched the travel shows Grandpapa used to watch. Eventually Dennis went to bed thinking the travel shows were boring and wondering where Grandpapa was traveling in the afterlife.

Dennis woke up midmorning on that Sunday as Mother shoved the breakfast dishes into the dishwasher. "I left you something to eat in the refrigerator," she told him. "Your sisters and I are going to the funeral home to take care of things."

"I don't need to eat. I want to go with you." Dennis did not want to stay in the house with maybe Grandpapa's ghost hanging around. More importantly, he wanted to help plan the funeral for a person he had grown fond of.

"You're too young and you'll get in the way. You can stay home with your father," Mother finalized her decision as she herded the sisters out the door.

"I think we got the better deal," Papa said from the kitchen table. "Let's play video games on the good TV. I'll take parental control off."

In a few days, Grandmother and Mother cremated Grandpapa since an urn was cheaper than a coffin. But they did have a brief ceremony, which seemed odd to Dennis just to bury a jar of ashes.

It was a cloudless, warm day when they all crowded into an unadorned, concrete building sitting in the middle of a cemetery without head stones. Dennis thought the square gray building looked strange sitting alone in the middle of a manicured lawn.

Inside, they all gathered in front of black steel drawers geometrically arranged in a granite wall. Dennis figured geometry must be important to housing ashes.

Mother stood next to her mother with the sisters on the other side. Dennis stood opposite of his sisters next to Papa. Grandmother's canasta players were scattered around in the background, as if not sure what side to choose.

One lower drawer hung open as the funeral director, a stranger to Grandpapa and the family, placed a dark blue urn inside. To Dennis, it looked like a pot to grow flowers. The pastor from Mother's church stood in front of the drawer, making it hard to see the urn. He talked mostly about the church's membership drive.

Dennis thought the funeral director closed the drawer pretty fast with a slam and a loud click. As if it would help Mother and Grandmother forget Grandpapa faster. With all the screaming and crying when he was alive, there was none of this by the sisters when Grandpapa was ashes closed forever inside a drawer.

Back at Grandmother's house for the reception, Mother's and Grandmother's women friends seemed to celebrate the demise of another man in the world. Dennis thought it sad that his grandpapa had no friends to come to his funeral. Maybe they were not told, he thought.

Heading toward the food, the sisters confronted Dennis in a narrow hallway. They blocked his way to the dining room.

"We're helping Mom and Grandma get rid of the old man's stuff," said Sarah.

"The old man is our grandpapa. Why are you getting rid of his stuff? Maybe I might want some of it," said Dennis.

"You need to stay out of this," warned Glenda.

"All that will be left when we're done is the old man's ghost," said Wendy, with an ugly smirk.

They stomped away, letting Dennis get his plate of food to take with him as he left with Papa back to their house. In the car, Dennis lost his appetite.

He thought more about Mother's resentment toward her father. Maybe, he considered, it wasn't about Grandpapa kissing a man, but kissing someone who was not Grandmother.

At home, Dennis was not worried about Grandpapa's ghost hanging around. Why stay around a place where he wasn't wanted when alive?

Back at Grandpapa's house, Grandmother, Mother, and his three sisters threw away what remained of Grandpapa's presence in the world. Family secrets erased forever. To die carelessly among surviving members. At least, that was what they thought.

Dennis sat at the kitchen table as Papa read his day-old newspaper. Pulling out his spiral notebooks with Grandpapa's secrets, Dennis looked at Papa and wondered what secrets were on his side of the family.

Rototillers and Older Sisters

Almost a year after Grandpapa's death and on a Thursday morning toward the end of summer, eleven-year-old Dennis watched his mother drive his three older sisters to an outdoor mall for a shopping trip. They were going for the sale specials to get ready for school. They left without asking Dennis to come along.

Mostly because he hid in his treehouse to avoid going. Shopping with his sisters would have been torture, even though his clothes were fitting tighter. He hoped his mother picked some clothes for him so he wouldn't have to go shopping.

When they got home a few hours later, the clothes Dennis's mother picked were not something he would wear unless he had to.

The next Thursday when they left, their shopping had evolved. Dennis overheard his sisters chattering away about meeting their friends. Even his mother had friends she was meeting. Dennis wished he could go along and learn about making friends. But it probably would have included shopping.

After they left, Papa came in from working in his garden. During the week, he worked ten-hour days, giving him an extra day off each week. Lately, he took it on Thursdays when he could be alone after his wife and daughters went for their shopping trip.

After cleaning up and with Dennis following him around, Papa dropped his son off at the library. Being among books always made Dennis happy. Papa went to have coffee with his friends, leaving Dennis to read books about making friends.

The next Thursday after the four of them left, Papa told Dennis, "You should have enough library books to keep you busy this morning. I need to do some work in the garage."

Before Dennis could say he read all of his books, Papa walked out the back door to the garage. Leaving an eleven-year-old in an empty house was not the safest thing for his papa to do, Dennis figured. Maybe he wants me to help him? Dennis thought this was more likely.

He found his papa kneeling in front of an old rototiller, concentrating on making random adjustments between the two-cycle engine and tines. Maybe hoping the two pieces of machinery would keep working together.

He decided to help his papa and handed him tools like pliers and wrenches. They made Dennis's fingers feel greasy.

"Papa, what tool do you need now?"

Papa didn't answer. Dennis guessed it would have broken his papa's concentration as he tried to loosen a rusted nut.

"Adjustable wrench," he said finally. Dennis thought Papa sounded like a doctor doing open heart surgery.

Dennis gave him the wrench with one hand and a small hammer with the other, thinking a few whacks on the nut would help. Papa ignored the offered hammer. Dennis put it back.

"Hammer," Papa said.

Dennis gave him the hammer and listened to Papa's grunts from struggling with the nut. He circled his papa, trying to see what tool he would need next when they bumped legs.

Stumbling backward, Dennis threw his greasy hands behind him while trying to keep his clean pants off the garage floor. His greasy hands made him slide more and he kicked out with his legs for balance. He kicked Papa's butt, who lost his balance and tipped the rototiller over in his effort not to.

The exposed tines looked like a laughing skeleton. To break the silence of Papa sitting on the garage floor with the upside-down rototiller next to him, Dennis suggested they buy a new one. Papa gave Dennis a look that meant he should leave.

As Dennis backed out of the garage, Papa struggled to right the rototiller. Dennis saw grease splotches on his papa's trousers. He thought Mother would be proud that he kept his pants clean.

Since he had nothing else to do, Dennis took the opportunity to sneak into his sisters' bedroom. Maybe there was something there that could help him figure out his sister's friendships that he could use for himself. Also, he thought it was time he learned something about these people who were a lot different from him.

He pushed open his sisters' bedroom door and flipped on the overhead light. Across the long room, Dennis was shocked at the quantity of female shaped clothing scattered across the floor and beds. The day before had been laundry day for the sisters. Mother's rule did not include putting the clothes away.

Dennis's laundry day was when he ran out of clothes or they smelled too much. Like his sisters, he helped wash his clothes, which was why his pants and shirts had bleached splotches.

Scanning the female clothing, Dennis figured it was no wonder Papa couldn't afford a new rototiller. Also, he understood why it took his sisters so long to pick school outfits. They had too many choices. He didn't have many clothes and most of them looked the same.

Dennis shuffled to Wendy's bed first, since it was by the door. Two years older than him at thirteen, he could picture her curly red hair, rigid jawline, and piercing brown eyes warning him not to touch her neatly folded clothes lying across her crisply made bed. Dennis was afraid just breathing around Wendy's bed would leave evidence he was there.

The next bed was Glenda's. Four years older than him with dark eyebrows and a long, straight nose, she left unfolded clothes split between bed and floor as if she enjoyed rejecting things. A hump under the covers of her bed was probably another quantity of clothes, or maybe the body of her latest boyfriend.

His oldest sister Sarah, a high school senior at seventeen, had the messiest situation with the most colorful clothes. Ever since seeing Grandpapa dead, she had gone from dark clothing to bright colors like blues and yellows.

Tall and thin, she had clothes and shoes piled around her unmade bed like a mountain to be climbed. Better not get too close, Dennis figured. He could trip and be buried alive.

Looking across their room, he saw that they each had individual spaces larger than his room. They even had their own extra-large bathroom. Dennis was not going in there. He did not want to find something female that they used in places he did not want to think about.

Standing in the middle of their room and still curious about these people, Dennis figured his sisters' five drawer dresser would be a good, safe place to look around. He pulled open the second drawer from the top, the first one he could see into.

He could not figure out who owned the lacy underwear. Dennis did not know why he touched lacy things. He tried to pull his fingers out and they just ended up tangled in the silkiness.

He panicked and shook his hand free, leaving a clump of twisted, slippery material as evidence he had been there. Dennis left the bedroom as fast as he could, hoping the hurriedness would help cover up any evidence he was there.

At noon, he heard his three sisters and Mother come home. Listening to the chattering and chaos of rustling shopping bags, he remembered he had left the bureau drawer open.

Panic came right into Dennis's throat as he heard his sisters pile into their bedroom, still chattering away, like a flock of crows cawing at each other for attention. He stepped into the hallway near their door and heard someone shove the drawer closed without comment. Dennis swallowed that hardness in his throat and vowed not to go snooping in there again.

The next Thursday and with school starting in a week, Mother and his sisters left to meet their friends again. Dennis approached Papa in the garage.

Papa quickly said he did not need any help. Dennis figured he needed to concentrate on getting the two-cycle engine and tines talking to each other before the weeds robbed his garden of life. He noticed that the stains on Papa's trousers had not washed off. With nothing else to do, Dennis went back into his sisters' bedroom.

Each of them had a vanity. Wendy's was so neat he didn't think she used it. Sarah's was too messy to go near. He approached Glenda's vanity and noticed she used a lot of makeup. More than the others.

He didn't understand what was wrong with her face that she needed to paint it. He studied Glenda's tubes, canisters, and brushes without touching any of them. Somehow, she and his other sisters seemed to connect with each other through this makeup and clothing to create an attraction different from their real self.

Dennis wondered what it would feel like to fix his body so that people noticed him and not who he was. Maybe that was what friendship was about.

He walked out of the room slowly, knowing he wouldn't be found out. There was no one to see him come or go from this room across the hallway from his. No one who was curious enough about him to have an interest in what he did. He climbed into his treehouse to read about the latest author he discovered recently, Jules Verne.

When his sisters came home, all three marched outside to his treehouse. They yelled up at him to stay out of their room. He forgot to close their door.

That Saturday afternoon, Glenda became fifteen like a runaway locomotive smashing through a warehouse made of glass. Mother chaperoned the birthday party that filled the house with giggling and shrieking girls. Papa helped by taking Wendy and Sarah to the movies; a romance adventure which were two words Dennis didn't think went together.

He helped by staying in his bedroom reading a Ray Bradbury book. He wanted to be in his treehouse, except it was raining. Violently, his bedroom door started shaking from heavy pounding.

He nearly fell on the floor. Dennis snatched the door open before he wouldn't have a door to open.

"You're a boy. You think boys will be attracted to this body of mine and like me?"

Glenda glared at Dennis, who only hoped one day to be taller than any of his sisters.

"What about your party?" Dennis could hear people singing Happy Birthday in the dining room.

"They don't need me. They know the words. Are boys going to like me?" Glenda whipped her long brown hair behind her as if she wanted to whip Dennis until he found her a boyfriend.

Predictions like this had no meaning to Dennis. "Yeah, of course boys will like you. Why wouldn't they? Didn't you say you had boyfriends already?"

"They weren't actually real or knew I was calling them my boyfriend."

Dennis did not like this situation. Glenda sought his brotherly advice on a topic he did not understand himself. "Boys will probably like you because you're a girl and you don't have too many pimples on your face."

"I know what I want." Glenda leaned her pimpled face toward Dennis. "It's to have a steady boyfriend before I graduate high school. If I can't do it on my own, I expect you to help."

She spun around and left as the singing died down. Dennis shut his bedroom door, trying not to picture Glenda with someone he knew.

The next morning was Sunday, yet the family had stopped going to church. After Grandpapa's death, mother resented a church preaching love for all, yet did not love who her father had been.

Mother explained to the family how she was the only one who could not love him for what he was or what he did. She was not against men liking men or women liking women or something in between. She didn't like her father not being faithful.

Dennis thought things were more relaxed without the stress of getting to church and believing in something they all had different opinions about. Dennis thought church people seemed to care more about church society than believing in God.

At the kitchen table, Dennis found Glenda reading Stephen King's *Christine*. He imagined the evil car, driven by a maniac Glenda, running him down over and over because he couldn't find her a suitable suitor.

To avoid Glenda, Dennis went to the garage where Papa was beaming with pride. "My rototiller is working like new. I want you to be the first to use it in the garden."

"You want *me* to operate *your rototiller*?" Dennis wondered if Papa had breathed in too many exhaust fumes from the rototiller engine. The smell hung in the stale garage air.

Papa pushed the rototiller toward the struggling garden in the back. Dennis followed, more from curiosity. Months before, he had watched Papa hunt for spots where soil and plants could work best with each other. Papa understood non-human things, including the rototiller, plants, and soil, much better than people. So it seemed to Dennis.

It was hot in the sun as Papa yanked hard on the starter rope. After the third pull, the engine sputtered to life with a cloud of wispy black smoke. A happy conclusion of engine and tines sang in the hot, humid air.

"Just drive it between the rows of plants," Papa instructed Dennis.

Dennis was overcome, overwhelmed, and overhappy. His papa believed in him enough to run this important machine so near to the plants he nursed to life.

Standing behind the handlebars, Papa showed his son how to engage the tines. Beneath Dennis's sweaty palms, the vibrating machine abruptly took off, digging into the hard, dry dirt.

Papa had placed the plants with enough space for the rototiller to cut between them. The machine dragged Dennis along between the rows as if it knew where it was going. This was good since Dennis barely kept the rototiller and himself upright and running away, taking him with it.

Through his sweaty haze, he glanced at the tomato vines and dangling pea pods. He wondered how far the watermelon vines would grow and he tried to understand why cabbage balls were not oblong. Dennis wondered at how living things could erupt to life from such an inhospitable land of soil.

He admired Papa's talent to mother plants and bring them to life from the hard dirt. Letting the tiller pull him along, he heard his father shout encouragement. Dennis felt an immense happiness that his papa was cheering him on.

At the end of the first row, Dennis managed to turn the machine around and head down another row of plants toward his papa. He hit a few rocks, but kept the rototiller from destroying any plants. Dennis figured hitting rocks would dull the tines and make Papa happy to have something to fix.

In the heat of summer and under the solitude of a hot sun, Dennis felt the ground beat back. As he approached the end of the row, Glenda stood there beside Papa.

With her hands on her hips, she looked like Superwoman. Dennis did not want to talk to her again about boys. He was still traumatized by yesterday's conversation. He wished he knew someone, but he had a friendless relationship at school. As he came to the end of the row where Glenda stood, she yelled to take a turn.

Papa nodded that it was okay. Dennis's arms were tired, any-way. With the tines disengaged but the engine running, Papa helped him turn the rototiller around toward another row before Glenda took the handlebars.

She braced herself and engaged the tines, wiping out the first tomato plant. Dennis didn't think the plant looked that healthy, anyway. With worry across her face, she glanced back at Papa, who waved Glenda on with a smile and a thumbs up.

Determined, she heaved the machine back between the rows of plants and kept going as if that rototiller was a boyfriend she demanded love from.

He watched her break the soil into pieces the plants could use to save themselves. His sister made it back without wiping out any more plants and with beads of sweat dangling across her forehead. One drop fell off the tip of her nose.

Papa had a big smile as Glenda went down another row. Den-nis thought about finding her a boyfriend. He might be okay with her dating someone he knew after all.

He wondered if Glenda would pick a person out for him, too. Watching her struggle with the rototiller, he saw her as the most spontaneous, passionate, and determined of his three sisters. That was why, when it came time to liking girls, he would pick his own.

Just Average

At twelve-years-old and in the seventh grade, school had become easier for Dennis. In the first semester of his last year of middle school, he surprised himself by making honor roll.

"What do you mean you didn't try? I try and I don't make honor roll." Glenda poked Dennis with her finger, then pointed at the laptop screen showing the results.

On the kitchen table, Mother had opened Dennis's grades and gathered everyone around to see. As if she needed witnesses.

"I made honor roll two grades before you," Wendy said, walking away.

"Being on the honor roll is so overrated," said Sarah, following Wendy.

"I want you to keep this up," Mother warned Dennis, pointing at the screen.

Papa patted Dennis on the back as if petting a dog. "Good work."

Mother and Papa walked away, leaving Dennis facing Glenda, who had jealousy written on her face.

"Don't worry about me being on the honor roll again. I don't want all this attention," said Dennis.

"Stop being ridiculous. You're probably smarter than all of us. Well, maybe not Wendy. But I don't like it, anyway." Glenda followed her sisters out of the kitchen.

In January when school started, Dennis was getting nervous and stressed out about attending junior high in September for the first time. His sisters did not help by telling him the drama they experienced in a place where everyone started puberty at the same time.

Also, he did not like the attention he got by being on the honor roll last semester. He imagined the drama he would experience being on the honor roll in junior high with developing teenagers.

To prepare, Dennis decided that, in his last five months of middle school, he would keep a C average in at least one class. It could bring notice to his pretend failure if he failed too much with too low of a grade.

It became a challenge to calculate the number of quizzes, tests, and projects to keep a C average. It was too easy to make As.

Despite this, near the end of the school year in early spring, he had successfully kept at least one C average through the interim reports. If he gained a better grade in one class, he fell in another. This method kept him outside teachers' attention with no honor roll stardom. Good practice for eighth grade, he thought.

On a Sunday evening in late May, Glenda pounded on Dennis's bedroom door. He opened it before she knocked it down.

"You're deliberately getting low grades to keep off the honor roll," she said, standing with her hands on her hips.

"You don't know that. Maybe I'm not as smart as everyone thinks," Dennis said. He wished he knew how Glenda had discovered his plan.

"You're smart enough to figure out how to stay off the honor roll." Glenda had a smirk.

"Being on the honor roll is not necessary to graduate high school," said Dennis.

"Fine, I don't care what you do. If you don't want to be on the honor roll when you deserve to be there, then that's your choice. Maybe it will help you cope with high school next year," said Glenda. "But this fall starts my last year of high school and it's got to be my best."

Dennis was ending middle school and none of his time there he would consider his best. They were just average. "Why do you need a best year and what does this have to do with me?"

"I want to end high school in a positive way and I don't want you embarrassing me."

"I haven't even got there yet and you're complaining. Wendy doesn't seem to care."

"Wendy has more confidence in herself. It's almost unnatural to me. It makes me feel so immature." Glenda stuck her lip out like a pout.

Dennis silently agreed with Glenda about Wendy. It was the same with Sarah.

"Anyway, how could I embarrass you?" Dennis could think of several things right away that he did not dare mention to Glenda and give her more reason to complain.

"Such as not having any friends. Every afternoon I watch you waiting for your bus and not talking to anyone. I don't want to be known as someone with the loner brother. High school is ruthless and you've got to make friends in junior high or people will think you're weird."

"Maybe I like being weird."

"Why don't you want to have friends? That's weird."

He wouldn't dare admit to Glenda that, basically, people scared him. Also, he still hadn't figured out how the friendship thing worked. Everyone he met either did not like the books he read or were just mean.

"I have friends. I just don't talk to them all the time like you do," Dennis said.

"That's not how friendship works. You need to talk to people more than you do. You'll need a support system in high school," said Glenda.

Dennis thought junior high school would be hard enough without trying to make friends and support a support system. "I'll be fine. You stay with your friends and I'll stay away. No one will know we're related."

"We are related. You can't avoid that. Do something about yourself or you'll end up like me getting out in the world and not sure who's your friend."

"Are you're afraid you'll end up with no friends after high school?" Dennis was confused.

"You're ridiculous. I can make friends anywhere. Just go ahead then and stand in that parking lot alone waiting for your old school bus." Glenda spun around, flipping her long, brown hair off her shoulders like a saber cutting off further conversation.

She left before Dennis could tell Glenda that he resented the friends she had made. When they came to the house, he never liked how they talked to his sister, as if they were not really her friends. Dennis decided he would not use Glenda's method of making friends, whatever that was.

That Monday afternoon, Dennis waited at school for his bus to come back after dropping off the first load of kids. As usual, he tried to avoid the middle school kids who had too much energy after sitting in school all day. Eventually, a teacher came by to say a minor accident would make the buses late.

Concerned about rising youthful energy levels, a few teachers came out to referee a tag football game. With one ball, one field, and a limited time before the buses returned for their second run, there could only be one game.

The teachers encouraged everyone to play, meaning everyone had to come to the field next to the parking lot. The only ones choosing not to play were several girls and a few boys who disliked sports and said they would cheer. Dennis didn't know how to cheer, so he figured he would stay in for a few plays before sneaking away.

The teachers picked the team captains—two boys who were natural leaders based on their out-of-control ego and love-me attitude, which the girls liked. They also had the potential to be cruel dictators one day.

The two boys raced through the selection process until it got down to skinny Cliff, too tall Hank, and Dennis. The team captains hesitated. Dennis figured he had a good chance to be selected next since he was average and not like one of those non-average boys he stood with.

The Team Left captain selected Hank, saying he was tall enough to block something before he tripped over his feet and fell. Team Right captain took Cliff muttering about being skinny enough that no one could tag him even though he was the slowest runner. Dennis stood alone.

The selection process abruptly ended as one of the teachers flipped a coin to see who got the ball first. Dennis stood there, forgotten. He wanted to be unnoticed, but not like this. Maybe my freckles are too freckly, he worried. A teacher with a frustrated look, as if it was Dennis's fault, pointed for him to go to Team Left.

Dennis trotted toward the Team Left captain, who told him to go to Team Right. When he got to Team Right, the captain had already surrounded himself with trusted agents and ignored Dennis.

Team Left took the ball first and made it halfway up the field with four complete passes. Each time, Dennis moved around on defense with Team Right players, looking for an escape. The cheer section formed a line between him and the school parking lot, blocking that escape.

After the fifth complete pass, Dennis saw a break in the cheer line where he could slip off the field and behind the teachers standing guard. One more pass, even if it was incomplete, and Dennis figured he could go that way with no one noticing.

As the Team Left captain took the ball, Dennis trotted back on defense close to his escape route. Boys and girls ran back and forth in front and behind him, waving their hands in the air to catch or block the ball if it came their way. Dennis stood in one place and raised his hands over his head like the others, not caring where the ball was thrown.

He figured it would go behind him, since that was where everyone ran. Dennis reached on his tiptoes to make it seem like he was really trying hard to block the pass as he kept his eye on his path to escape. Except, just as the Team Left captain threw the ball, he slipped on the grass.

Too tall Hank, chased by skinny Cliff, ran in front of Dennis and momentarily blocked his view of the ball. After they ran past, something slapped into his outstretched hands. Dennis pulled it down to his chest.

He looked down at the muddy football, wishing it was someone's wet underwear. Everyone stopped running and stared at Dennis. No one knew whose side he was on.

Since most of the people were behind him and he did not want to be tagged standing there, Dennis ran away from them toward the opposite goal line.

He crossed the scrimmage line and kept running toward the Team Right goal, with just a few kids standing between him and a touchdown. What would he do if he scored? All he could think of was to keep running. Maybe the end of the universe would happen very, very soon, he hoped.

Dennis felt a push on his back knocking him face forward into the wet grass. He let go of the football, trying to keep from getting grass stains. It didn't work and he got up to watch boys and girls from both teams, who had been chasing him, run like a mob after the loose football that went skidding away on the wet grass.

He waited for someone to say "nice interception" or "way to go." Instead, the Team Right players recovered the football.

No one said anything as Dennis walked off the field in his grass-stained clothes. He did not care who saw him leave. One play later, Team Right players scored the only touchdown of the game off his interception.

Dennis did not see it. Instead, he heard the cries of delight coming from girls and boys at that end of the field. He sat on the parking lot curb throwing pebbles at the spot where the bus would eventually pick him up.

"It was a nice interception." Glenda stood next to Dennis.

"You saw?" Dennis sat with grass-stained pants.

"To be honest, one of my girlfriends came to pick up her brother since the buses were late. I thought I should do the same. Even if you don't have any friends."

"Thanks, but I can wait for the bus."

"That's dumb. Come on." Glenda offered her hand to help her brother up.

He took it. Maybe it was better I was not the hero of the game, he thought. It would be too much attention. He smiled at Glenda, happy his sister was giving him a ride home.

Shelf Life

One Saturday morning in early September after Dennis started junior high school, Papa drove off in his pickup, pulling a rented horse trailer. Dennis was still adjusting to the five-acre farm his parents bought in late summer, although his sisters were happy. The house gave them separate bedrooms and a larger bathroom. Dennis's bedroom and bathroom shrank.

Watching him drive away, Dennis wondered if Papa was picking up something to save the neglected farmland. During the coming fall and winter, he wanted to get the land ready for planting next spring. Dennis thought it would take a lot to get the soil ready for anything.

The first time thirteen-year-old Dennis saw Papa's farm, even the weeds struggled to grow there. He believed the only way Papa could prepare the land was by replacing it with fertile land from some place else. He wondered if that was what Papa planned to do with the trailer.

In the back of the house on the other side of a wide backyard were two buildings. One was a long open-sided shed hosting a small tractor and equipment the tractor could pull and maybe save the land. There was no room for the rototiller and no real use for it on the large farm.

Dennis wished they could have kept the rototiller. But Papa found a better home for it at a local non-profit who planted small community gardens. Dennis thought the rototiller would be great to help people grow food as long as they had someone working on it all the time.

The other building was a loft barn with two wide stalls.

The barn sagged in different directions. If Dennis looked at it front ways, it appeared to lean forward. When he looked sideways, it seemed to lean backward. Dennis thought the only thing keeping the barn standing was that you could not tell which direction it would fall.

Dennis wasn't sure what Papa was going to use the barn for. Two hours later, he found out.

Papa came back with a black and white Holstein cow in the horse trailer. Its udder was so swollen that Dennis worried the sack could burst at any moment. Great, another female, he thought.

Dennis, his sisters, and Mother made a human fence circling the cow beast as Papa led it toward the barn. The tall cow gave Dennis a sideways get-lost look. It was the same one he got from his sisters. Obviously, all female mammals had that universal look, he decided.

With heavy, clumpy steps and no concern for the human bystanders, the cow lumbered in a slow arc into the barn. There, a stall waited with fresh sawdust on the floor and a trough of fresh hay hanging on the wall that she grabbed a mouthful of, as if she had always lived there.

Mother and the sisters retreated into the house, chattering loudly about the trail of runny manure the cow left on its way to the barn. They complained even louder about how the money for the cow could have bought them new clothes and shoes.

Dennis thought the cow was better than clothes and shoes. Although, a cow probably contributed to at least the shoes. Besides, the manure would make good fertilizer for the ground.

Papa stepped into the narrow stall, unperturbed about being in a small place with a large cow. He put a tin pail under the cow's udder and sat on a short wooden stool he brought along. Dennis lost sight of his papa behind the cow's bulging stomach.

Quickly, Dennis heard a squishy, splattering, ringing sound against the pail's insides. Like someone having a hard time peeing. With his curiosity overwhelmed, Dennis kneeled into the soft sawdust beside his papa.

Under the cow's belly, he watched Papa use his hand and fingers to gently pull down on one of the long teats. At the climax of the pull, a belch of reddish-whitish fluid squirted out into the pail. Papa immediately repeated the process with his other hand on the opposing teat creating a careful rhythm.

The Holstein twisted her enormous head toward the two and gave them both a snort of hot breath. One move by the cow and it would be crushville for him and Papa, Dennis thought. But the Holstein didn't seem to care enough about them. Papa continued to squirt milk as the cow turned back to the more interesting trough of hay.

"You've watched long enough. Here, grab this teat up high and carefully let your fingers roll down to the end," Papa told his son.

The sawdust felt soft under Dennis's knees as he fumbled for the elongated protrusion dangling from the swollen udder. He wanted to know where his papa learned to milk a cow. The Holstein turned her head again to watch this newbie and Dennis wondered which direction cows kicked.

Unexpectedly, Dennis caught his father's scent. The left-over after-shave from the morning or maybe the beads of sweat taking up residence on his forehead. Dennis hunched beneath the cow's stomach as Papa guided his son's hands toward a teat.

Dennis lightly braced his long fingers at the top and he let Papa guide his fingers like a rolling pin downward. A tug at the end brought a weak squirt of milk that pinged the side of the tin pail.

"It doesn't look white," Dennis said, trying to concentrate on the next squeeze. He worried he had squeezed too hard.

"We won't use this first batch. It has blood in it. She had a calf recently and she's been moved around too much. Maybe on the third or fourth milking we can pasteurize and keep the milk. It'll be good for some hot chocolate."

"What are you going to do with today's milk?"

"I'm going to dump it in the field as fertilizer."

Papa turned the closest teat toward his son. He pushed out a weak squirt of milk that hit Dennis on his chin. They both laughed as the cow turned her head to make sure they were not laughing at her. Dennis always remembered this one moment with his papa.

With Papa's help, Dennis got better with the pulling and squirting. When they finished, they carried the cow's bloody milk into a corner of the field where even the weeds had gone into a coma like state. Dennis thought that if the field had any hope for next spring, it would be from the bloody milk.

For the next week, Dennis milked the Holstein every morning before school and afternoon when he got home. The more Dennis got to know the cow, the more he felt like a bond was growing between them.

Sometimes when milking, the cow would turn to watch Dennis and give a vicious snort from both large nostrils, spraying him with cow boogers. Dennis thought it was like the animal was blowing him a kiss. A very messy, yucky one.

Since he had no friends in school, and his sisters were more like aliens from space, the cow had become his only friend. Therefore, he decided she needed a name. The only one he could think of was Shelf Life.

He figured the cow's milk would eventually have a long shelf life when it cleared up. Now with a name, Shelf Life became someone Dennis could continue to care for. Even if the cow barely tolerated Dennis with all its snorting. After several weeks, Dennis worried about the nights getting colder for Shelf Life.

"We need to get some heat for her," Dennis announced at supper one Friday night. Mother had made hamburgers.

"She'll be alright as long as we keep the doors and windows closed. I put her in that stall where she'll get the most sun." The juice from Papa's hamburger dripped over his fingers.

"Maybe we can get her some blankets when it gets too cold. Also, when is the milk going to be good enough to pasteurize and drink?" Dennis was not interested in his burger.

All three sisters and Mother explained loudly how they were not drinking the cow's milk, no matter how pasteurized it was. Dennis said nothing because he wasn't sure he'd drink it, either.

Papa kept quiet and Dennis wondered why he brought Shelf Life home if it wasn't to drink her milk.

The next morning as Dennis milked Shelf Life, he told the cow, "I decided Papa brought you here because he likes your milk fertilizing his field. You're his secret formula to grow a crop next year. So, you'll need to make a lot more milk."

Shelf Life stopped munching on hay, turned toward Dennis, and gave one moo before going back to eating. As if Shelf Life knew something else was coming.

Dennis continued pulling on each tapered teat in a rhythm that had become natural to him. The milk in the tin pail continued to look like he had squeezed pieces of Shelf Life's inner udder out with the milk.

Once, Glenda tried to explain to him about her period and how pieces of her came out with the blood. Dennis didn't want to hear about all those disgusting female things. He knew the issue with Shelf Life could not be the same.

Sometimes as Dennis sat on the wooden stool, he played games with the reddish stream shooting out from the teats. He made whirlpools and pretended the pail was a turbulent universe made peaceful by a tin pail of reddish milk. He made planets by causing bubbles to form on the surface.

One Sunday morning, Glenda appeared in the barn's doorway silhouetted against the rising sun. "You just like pulling on her teats for therapy. You think that cow is your friend and that's pathetic. If it was a girl, she'd hate you."

She was right on that, which Dennis refused to admit. He hated Glenda knew that much about him. "Why aren't you hanging out with your high school friends today?"

"We had a fight. Anyway, this is my last hear in high school. When I get to college, I can have different friends."

"What did your friends do to you?" Dennis got angry with her friends.

"It's nothing. We'll get over it. It's what friends do."

"I don't think I want friends if they're like that." Dennis kept milking.

"Look, I just came to see if you needed any help." Glenda stepped further into the barn.

"You want to milk Shelf Life?" Dennis was never sure what his sisters wanted. They were confusing.

Glenda said nothing, but walked over and kneeled beside her brother. He wasn't sure what was happening. But he felt good sharing what he knew with his sister.

She sat on the stool while he sat on the sawdust. He showed his sister about pulling on swollen teats.

Dennis guided Glenda's hand as she pulled. But she yanked too hard, like she was thinking about her friends and Dennis worried she was hurting Shelf Life. Also, he had yet to find out what direction cows kicked. Shelf Life mooed in warning while still eating.

He guided Glenda's fingers carefully onto another teat. Dennis smelled Glenda's sweat that had become sweeter the last few years while his other sister's smell becoming sourer. She got two weak squirts out.

Dennis knew his sister had the hang of it and the next squirt would be perfect. He was proud he was sharing something with his sister. Before Glenda could get the good squirt out, her smartphone sang some pop song.

She abruptly stood, ripped out her smartphone from her pocket, and erupted in a big "hi" while walking away. Glenda talked excitedly about making up with her friends.

She left without saying anything more to her brother, who went back to milking Shelf Life. Maybe Glenda's sweat did smell just as sour as the others, he decided.

Dennis finished milking and dumped the bloody milk in a new spot in the field. Where he had dumped the milk before already had weeds perking up as if getting drunk on the blood. There was hope for Papa's field, he thought.

By late fall, Dennis thought it possible he would make it through high school without too much trauma as long as Shelf Life was around. He just wished she would stop with the bloody milk.

On a Friday evening in the middle of November, Dennis stepped off the school bus and headed toward the barn. He bypassed the lit up house, planning to tell Shelf Life she would be the subject of his first writing assignment. Inside the barn, Dennis confronted an empty stall.

"Where is she?" Dennis stood just inside the kitchen doorway watching Mother chopping vegetables. Dennis sensed Papa's absence. Glenda, who hated homework, sat at the kitchen table with her schoolbook opened in front of her. Wendy took her books out of the kitchen and Sarah, who had come home from college, stopped helping Mother and left the room.

"Your father can tell you when he gets back," Mother said without interrupting her chopping.

"No, I want to know now. I'm supposed to be milking her. She's expecting me." Dennis noticed Glenda was reading her book upside down.

"Calm down, Dennis." Mother cut up the vegetables more slowly. "She fell this morning and couldn't get up." She stopped chopping.

Dennis stared at her back as she ignored his staring. He saw his mother as empty as the stall in their barn. He clenched his fists at his sides as Mother made him not understand why he lived there among all these women.

She finally turned to face her son. "Please, wait until your father gets home. He wanted to explain it to you. He should have been home by now."

Glenda kept paying vivid attention to her upside-down textbook, except now tears were on her cheeks. The other two sisters kept staying away.

Dennis lost his position in time and space. He hoped his voice did not squeak. "I want Shelf Life back." The silence of the room pounded in Dennis's ears.

"Shelf Life was sick." Mother said in a soft voice, facing her son.

"She's been taken to the market to be killed and eaten as if she was never real. Isn't that it? Why? She wasn't sick. There was nothing wrong with her. All she did was let me milk her. I didn't even get to say goodbye."

Dennis stomped out of the house and slammed the front door. He ran to the barn where he stood in the middle of Shelf Life's stall. Looking around, he saw her manure mixed in the sawdust.

It looked runny and gooey. Evidence of her fate and fear, he decided. He wondered if Shelf Life cried.

"I didn't care that you didn't care about me," Dennis told Shelf Life's manure. "You were always there for me to milk and to talk to."

He stared into the slats of the stall just like Shelf Life did. The oak slats gave a view of the barn door where Dennis came twice a day. The tall windows brought sunshine in.

He remembered when he put a halter on and led Shelf Life across the field for exercise. She always laid runny manure everywhere before pulling Dennis back to her stall as if it was her safe place.

Dennis touched Shelf Life's leftover hay, imagining her standing right where he stood as he milked her. Turning around, he spied Glenda standing at the barn's entrance.

"I'm sorry about Shelf Life," she said. Her voice quivered and he could see she had been crying. "They won't take her to slaughter or eat her. It's like euthanasia."

She stumbled away, not waiting for Dennis's response. He had none, anyway. Dennis realized he stood in Shelf Life's manure. It stunk with flies buzzing around.

Half an hour later, he watched Papa drive up in the pickup without the rented trailer. Through the barn door, Dennis watched his papa go into the house and come out again, taking long steps toward the barn.

"Her milk never cleared because she was old and in pain." Papa stood in the barn doorway. The fading outside light caused his face to be in shadow. "Cows can only have eight births. She had nine."

"I could have taken care of her."

"I'm not having an animal suffer like that. I bought her because the owner was taking her to market and I thought she had a few more years. I'm sorry."

It was the first time Dennis ever heard his papa apologize.

Papa hesitated, as if drawing the courage to explain his apology. "I was wrong to bring Shelf Life here." They both stared at each other for a few moments before Papa turned and left.

Dennis followed him and took his shoes off at the back stairs since they stunk of Shelf Life's manure. The last trace of her person on Earth.

Supper was on the table and no one said anything to Dennis. Mother served spaghetti, his favorite. Dennis ignored it and went back to the barn to stare at the sawdust. He saw Shelf Life's hoof prints, some of the last marks she made in the world. Eventually, Glenda came out.

"I get it. Shelf Life was your best friend and now she's gone," she said.

"I should have at least said goodbye."

"You'll remember her, so it's not really goodbye."

She hugged Dennis for a long time. When they went back to the house, she had to wash Shelf Life's manure off her shoes, too.

That weekend, Dennis spent as much time as possible inside the barn where Shelf Life used to live. He imagined milking her and realized they had mice in the barn. The next Saturday morning, Glenda pounded on Dennis's bedroom door.

"I'm not getting up yet," Dennis shouted.

"We've got something to show you in the barn." Glenda pounded on the door again.

Dennis went with Glenda before she tore down his bedroom door. They headed out the back porch where Dennis saw Papa, Mother, and his two older sisters standing in front of the barn. Dennis eyed Glenda suspiciously.

"I don't want another cow. Nothing can replace Shelf Life," he said.

"Believe me, we're not making that mistake twice."

Inside the barn and standing in Shelf Life's stall on new sawdust was a short black and white animal.

"This is Mary. She was Shelf Life's last calf." Papa explained, "Shelf Life was used for dairy, so her calf was weaned from her after about two days. This means she was taken off her mother's milk and put on bottle-fed formula."

"She never knew her mother?" Wendy sounded worried.

"There are better ways to wean calves from their mothers than taking them away so young," said Sarah. She sounded angry, like she wanted a debate.

A good feeling came over Dennis. His family was all involved in this young calf standing before them, who decided at that moment to let out a long, noisy pee.

"She's almost eight months old and weighs close to five hundred pounds. So, don't let her step on you. The grain, hay, and corn silage we have will help her mature into an adult heifer. And I've installed a heater that won't catch the barn on fire but keep her warm," said Papa.

"When do we milk her?"

"When she has a calf in about a year and a half. She'll be a cow then," said Papa.

"Mary's not getting pregnant," said Dennis, in a tone that dared anyone to challenge him.

He and Mary eyed each other in agreement as the rest of the women in the family left. Papa stayed to show Dennis instructions on taking care of Mary.

That night he tried to sleep with Mary. Until she snorted in his face to let him know it was her stall.

In the coming years, Mary helped Dennis survive high school, college, and experiences with the female culture as he grew up during those times. He only shared Mary with the woman he would love forever.

Well, maybe Glenda, too. And maybe Wendy and Sarah.

Adventure with Papa

During her first year, Dennis took the heifer Mary out for afternoon walks in the field, like a dog. He thought her poop and pee had been excellent fertilizer so far and helped Papa's crops. Like her mother Shelf Life. However, in early December the cold convinced Mary she preferred the warmth of her stall that, after combining the two, was bigger than the room Dennis had.

The cold settled in like a winter habit, although snow and ice had still to visit. In that first week of cold and at supper on a Friday evening, Papa told Dennis that he would go with him in the morning.

"Where're we going?" Fourteen-year-old Dennis never knew his papa to take him anywhere without the sisters unless to the library. He hoped they were going to the new library annex in the next county.

"We're going to Farmer Jack Victory's farm. He's a client at the accounting firm and he needs our help early tomorrow morning." Papa did not look up from eating his pork chops.

"Jack is an important client. You can't mess anything up when you're there." Mother wiggled the end of her fork at Dennis for emphasis before going back to her pork chop.

Dennis didn't intend on messing anything up. He figured his mother was trying to teach him stress, but he already had enough of it with being in the ninth grade. Next year would be senior high and he had yet to figure out junior high. Now that Mother mentioned it, the thought of messing up in front of an important client of Papa's prayed on Dennis's mind like a fart, squirming to get out.

"I want to go," Glenda said. At eighteen, she was home from her first semester of college and always wanted to do whatever Dennis was doing.

"No, only your father and Dennis are going." Mother said. She chomped on a piece of pork off the end of her fork.

"Don't worry about me. I don't want to go," said sixteen-year-old Wendy.

"Neither do I," said twenty-year-old Sarah, also home from college. "Us girls should do some shopping instead."

"I want to go. Dennis is just gonna screw things up," said Glenda.

"Farmer Jack Victory decided who can come. It's his farm," said Mother.

"Dennis can fill you in when he gets back," said Papa to Glenda.

Glenda glared at Dennis and he thought he would have a hard time explaining anything to her, as angry as she looked. Really, he wished Glenda could come. Dennis was getting nervous not knowing what would happen, and she could at least share in his anxiety.

Dennis figured Papa needed to keep a wealthy customer happy, and only males were invited. This scared Dennis the most. He had spent his life with females and he wasn't sure exactly how to act when it was only males.

He ignored the rest of the conversation as he stared at the slab of pork on his plate. His entire life up to that point involved his sisters, which did nothing but make him worry about how to act when it was just Papa and him. He aimed his fork at the carrots.

Morning came suddenly when Papa turned Dennis's bedroom light on an hour and a half before sunrise. Dennis popped up in bed, thinking Glenda was attacking him.

"Get dressed. We're leaving in a few minutes," Papa said.

They left the house with everyone still sleeping. Papa drove in the cold darkness saying nothing and Dennis was glad. He had a nervous twitch in his stomach as he munched on a bologna and cheese sandwich his mother made the night before.

Dennis was glad for the silence since he probably would have said something stupid and started on his way to messing things up in front of his papa. The sandwich was his favorite, and he took his time eating it.

After twenty minutes, they turned down Farmer Jack Victory's dirt road, passing farm fields on both sides until coming to a rambler style house. The kitchen and porch lights shone through the moonless, pre-dawn darkness. As they approached, Farmer Jack Victory sat on the porch in a rocker with a heavy looking, coffee-stained mug in his hand and a white cigarette poking out of his mouth.

Papa and Jack nodded at each other in some type of ceremonial salute that Dennis failed to copy. He did not think he should be noticed this early in the relationship. Probably, the farmer did not think him noticeable, anyway.

Dennis hung back, trying to pick out details that would give him clues as to what he was doing there before sunrise. He didn't understand why Papa wouldn't tell him anything. Maybe he was protecting him from worrying about what would happen. Thinking about this made Dennis worry.

He heard a noise and turned around to see another pair of headlights negotiating the dirt road. It never occurred to Dennis that there might be others. He had strangers to mess up in front of.

Out of the dark car climbed Herb Janken and his son, high school junior, Leroy. Dennis knew Leroy enough from school gossip to know he did not want to know him. The junior inherited biased opinions from his father that Dennis had nightmares about.

Herb and Leroy stood shorter than Papa, but taller than Dennis. Herb had a pregnant looking belly and Leroy stood on weak, thin legs. They both had shallow jaw lines that made Dennis think about people with stumbling thoughts and misdirected ambitions.

They did not look that strong, despite their narrow-minded opinions. Dennis thought he had a chance. He shivered as he caught Farmer Jack Victory staring at him through the cold air, as if he was the only normal person there.

The farmer threw the remains of his coffee over the porch railing and into the darkness. He punished his cigarette butt into the arm of the chair and dumped it into the coffee cup he left in the seat. Without a word, the farmer led them all from the house, down a short hill, and toward a cinderblock building in the middle of a blank field.

Darkness surrounded them except for the dim lighting coming from the building. Grabbing a metal handle designed by some random beating of a hammer, the Farmer Jack Victory pulled open a large wooden door. They took turns stepping inside with Dennis last, like a priority thing. A flash of overhead, neon lights revealed their mission. That, of which, was to kill.

"I got a hog to be butchered, and we got to move fast before the sun heats the air. I don't want to get into a race with maggots," said the farmer.

They all stared at the assembly of slaughtering tools hanging on the room's walls. Dennis gazed at the array of sharp knives and short-handled axes with crisp points, and he wanted to run away. But it was dark and cold outside and he worried Leroy could throw one of the sharp tools at him for fun.

A walk-in freezer from ceiling to floor dominated the room. The rest of the place held a long stainless-steel table. "This is where we'll cut up the meat," said Farmer Jack Victory.

Before anyone could talk, he darted out of the building and led them along a short muddy path to a smaller cinder block building. There was a pretense at a wooden door the farmer almost pulled off the hinges as he yanked it opened.

Inside, they were bathed in bug encrusted neon lights revealing oak slats encircling the muddy home of a hog. The animal let out a startled squeal that sounded like a late-night horror movie.

Everyone approached with testosterone building. Except Dennis, who stood in the back of this male crowd, cautiously.

"I know it's time for a hog killin' when I start to see the bottom of my freezer. This hog is near to two hundred and ten pounds and 'bout five months old. Good 'nough 'though I like 'em to be over two hundred and twenty and slightly older."

Farmer Jack Victory stood staring at the big hog, which stared back at him. Like an executor facing the victim. The hog seemed too fat to get up from its squalor and fight for its life.

Dennis failed to avoid the animal's large, frightened eyes. Soon, it's organs would cease to function and its brain waves would stop waving. Dennis was about to take part in this murder, and being a vegetarian became more appealing. He wondered why Papa brought him as Papa and Herb pulled on rubber boots.

He envied Glenda. Right then she was cozy sleeping in bed quilts, probably dreaming about making herself prettier and more attractive to boys. He hoped one of the boys was not Leroy. Based on her selection of friends, Glenda already knowing Leroy concerned Dennis.

All five of them stared at the doomed hog. It stared back at them with sad, curled eyes. Its short ears drooped and it gave a quick snort from its long snout, causing dribble to fall into the muck it laid in.

"It's a Berkshire. One of the old-line breeds that's hardy and durable. You can tell with those white splashes of color on its black coat. It's a well muscled breed that's good for leanness and high yield," said the experienced farmer.

"That kind has got some premium pork in it," said Herb. "Got them large loin eye areas and finishes off good, I bet."

"It should be a high grade with good marbling." Papa said.

Dennis wondered where Papa learned about hogs. He hoped Leroy kept quiet or he would feel pressured to say something.

"They make pretty good fathers," said Leroy.

Were they supposed to have studied up on hogs? Dennis did not even know he would be here staring at an animal staring back at him with eyes pleading for clemency.

"This is a barrow. Not much at fathering without the right equipment," said Farmer Jack Victory.

Great, Leroy got one wrong. Although Dennis didn't know what a barrow was. He took this to mean the competition had ended.

"A few months ago, this suit guy tried to sell me a feeder pig I know weren't used for much. I could tell by looking at it that it wasn't much more than sixty or seventy pounds. That told me right there the animal was slow growing or stunted and weighing too much for its ten weeks of age," said the farmer.

Dennis experienced information overload. Suppose the farmer asked me questions later, like on a test, he thought.

"Look at this animal. It has good internal body dimensions. That makes for a hardier and efficient growth." The farmer pointed at different parts of the animal. It was like he was teaching a class.

"What's good efficiency?" Dennis blurted out the question, forgetting he wanted to stay unnoticed. The others seemed to know enough to keep quiet and listen to the lecture. Dennis let his curiosity take him to places of questions, like he did in school.

"Means it takes less feed to make the growth." Farmer Jack Victory said. "I've had hogs with daylight or coon footed. Lost you yet?"

"Yeah." Dennis spoke instinctively, before understanding sarcasm.

"If it has good leg length, then you can see daylight 'neath the pig. Raccoon footed hogs walk with a flatter foot and do better on concrete. Enough teaching. Time to get to working."

Sensing terror, the hog struggled to a standing position. Manure waste dripped off its underbelly, pooling underneath. As the farmer stepped toward the animal, it squealed and ran to the other end of the small inside pen as if knowing its fate.

Stepping into the shallow muck, the three men slowly surrounded the hog, forcing it into a corner of the pen. Leroy and Dennis stood outside rooting for their dads, well at least Leroy was rooting. Dennis was in shock at seeing his papa trying to corral a hog to kill it. It was comical, in a sad sort of way.

Eventually the hog stopped moving, surrounded and confused about which direction to escape. Farmer Jack Victory grabbed the animal's front feet like a ninja and flipped the hog on its back. A whistling squeal from the trapped hog saturated everyone's ears as muck splattered up and hit Dennis in his face. Leroy was faster and ducked behind Dennis.

The farmer pulled out two thick ropes and bound the front legs together, then hind legs in a blood cutting tie. Next, he pulled out a wicked metal hook long enough to snare the loop in the hind hooves. The three men dragged the squealing hog across the dirty brown muck and manure to the gate.

Leroy jumped in to help and immediately got in the way. Dennis was in position to do something, and he stepped back to get out of the way. They pulled the hog in front of Dennis, who only heard the awful high-pitched squealing.

Out of the pen, but still in the small shed, the farmer pulled out a thicker rope and threaded it through the hook's loop before slinging it over a pulley dangling over them. Dennis and Leroy grabbed some part of the struggling hog as the rest of the men grabbed the thick rope and hoisted the desperate animal upside down. The about-to-be-executed hog swung its gigantic head around, hitting Dennis and sending him to the floor.

He wallowed in the muck, thinking about his Mother's curse not to mess things up. Farmer Jack Victory reached over and pulled Dennis to a standing position while in his other hand he held a short saber of a knife. The sharpness glittered in the dull overhead neon lights.

"Get that gun off the wall," the farmer said, pointing to it.

Herb took the rifle off the pegs. "This is a .22."

"It's got long rifle bullets in it. Shoot at the center of my X on the hog's forehead." The farmer used his index finger to mark the spot.

Herb proudly gave the gun to Leroy, who swiftly placed the muzzle between the hog's eyes. Papa and Herb held the hog's head in a vise of muscle, almost bringing a moment of calm to the doomed animal. It seemed to accept its upside down, condemned position.

Dennis heard a quick pop from the gun as the hog shot its hoofs in four different directions at once while trying to squeal. Leroy ended up on the concrete floor, trying to stand. He had barely hit the hog's head. Dennis was glad he hadn't shot anyone.

As Papa and Herb struggled to stop the hog's twitching, Farmer Jack Victory jerked the rifle from Leroy, pointed it at the hog's forehead, and put one quick shot off. The sudden stillness from the hog's mass hung all around them as if the universe had died.

The farmer handed the rifle to Dennis, who did not know what to do with the murder weapon. He held it as Farmer Jack Victory swiped the short saber across the hog's exposed throat in one swift motion. Herb and Papa yanked the head up and back, bringing a torrent of blood plummeting out into a large pan the farmer shoved in place just in time.

They all stood in the stark quiet of the pre-dawn morning, listening and watching the hog's life blood dump into the galvanized pan. The moment lasted for several minutes as everyone stood in silence until the splattering slowed. Dennis was filled with sadness as the hog transitioned from life to death. He turned around and hung the rifle back on the wall.

Leroy stood there looking pale with a big dark stain on the seat of his pants. Soon, like a distant wood chime, a gurgle emitted from the hog's throat and sent the blood into a trickle.

Quickly, the farmer spit out orders as he swung a battered back door open to reveal burning hot fires outside. Dennis could see flames licking the rounded sides of a massive enamel bathtub. The boiling water breathed hot vapors into the cold air.

The pulley that the dead hog hung from came out of a steel arm that let them swing the carcass into the cold air and over the bathtub of scalding water. Blood drops left a splattered trail that Dennis carefully avoided as he followed the hanging animal.

The farmer used a come-along as a winch to sink the hog into the boiling water. The smell of charring wood and the odor of singed hog hair hit the inside of Dennis's nose at the same time. From then on, Dennis always associated burned hair with death.

After a few minutes, he joined the others to pull the steaming carcass onto a wooden table next to the bathtub. As they stood outside in the cold and dark, the farmer put a wide scraper into Dennis's hands. It felt surprisingly light and strong.

The others held scrapers, too, and they all began scraping the coarse hair off the tight hot skin. Dennis wasn't the best, but he thought he tried the hardest. Mostly because he wanted to get it over with as soon as possible and go home.

Farmer Jack Victory helped Dennis a few times in tough spots. No one said a word as their faces disappeared in the steam coming off the dead, shaven hog.

Dennis did not know how long they scraped. Only that it was suddenly over when the three men hoisted the bare hog onto a beaten metal cart with oversized rubber wheels. They wheeled the hairless animal down to the cinderblock building at a trot. Dennis followed, realizing there it was too dark to escape.

Inside the clean cinder block building, each of them helped lift the still warm, hairless hog onto the stainless-steel bench where the slaughtering began.

Papa shoved his son to the end with Leroy last. Butcher paper hung in a roll on the pegged wall in front of Dennis, and he realized he was in a good position to witness the gutting.

He thought the scene was like watching a romance movie in slow motion. The farmer sliced open the hog's front, from crotch to head, as Herb and Papa pulled the carcass open. The experienced farmer used a hatchet to finish breaking the thick breast bones. Dennis heard cracks like the snapping of tree branches in a bad storm. He tried to erase the grimace he felt on his face.

"Got no use for the pizzle, and you got to make sure the urinary tract is tied tight along with the anus. Don't want to taste piss or shit when you eat ham or pork." Farmer Jack Victory had an energy that made him sound like a young elementary school teacher just out of college.

With a smirk, he shook the pizzle at Dennis, who thought it looked like a penis. It went into a large vat at the table's feet before Dennis could be sure what it was.

Each entrail, formerly warm and well fed, slithered out the open slit, felt the cold air, and breathed with steam. Like a newborn taken from its mother. The farmer used the vat but also threw chosen body parts into a deep glass bowl of ice-cold water sitting on the steel table.

He used his two large, callused hands and most of his hairy arms to pull out the hog's torso cavity. To Dennis, it looked like the hog had vomited inside out. All he could make out were pink swollen clumps of organs and long tendrils of intestines and other tubular structures that he could not identify.

They all fell across the lip of the bench and into the large vat. "Gotta be careful here," the farmer said. "Any cut, tear, or puncture is gonna contaminate everything."

Everyone stayed silent, not wanting to cause the experienced farmer to make a mistake.

"Alright, folks. Let's cut up this carcass. Primal cuts first."

Dennis thought primal cuts sounded like cave-man primitive. He had no clue what they were as the cutting went into production line status.

He caught the cut-up parts in his chilly hands and wrapped each piece while Leroy did the tying and labeling. In his hands, Dennis could feel the warm meat and knew that the heat originated not from the hot bath, but when the hog was alive.

After they had been at it for a while, he spied sunlight peeking through the nearby pane glass window. It made everyone work faster and Dennis wondered why the farmer didn't air-condition the building.

Also, Dennis wondered why Farmer Jack Victory did not use a butcher shop that would have cut up the hog in a more sanitary place. Wrapping another piece of meat, he realized the hog butchering was some type of tradition the farmer wanted to experience again. An experience he wanted to share. Without children, the four of them were his legacy.

Dennis thought this while tiredness seeped through his body. He had no clue anymore what type of warm meat went through his hands. Only that he wished it would soon end.

It did end as the raw meat stopped heading Dennis's way. The hog was now no longer a hog, but so many wrapped parts in the freezer behind him. Dennis looked at the dirty red stains spilled across the silver table and wondered where Papa learned to cut up a hog.

The cleanup erased the remaining residue of the hog. It was like murderers cleaning up their murder site. Remnants of the hog went down the drain erasing any memory of the animal's existence. The hog was now just packaged meat, ready to be cooked and eaten.

After the cleanup, they followed the farmer back to the murder scene. Dennis worried if they were going to kill something else. They were now part of a secret club of hog killers and anything was possible.

Terrible as it seemed, they re-entered the building where the hog had lived its entire life among the muck and grime. This time, no animal cries rose out of the silent, empty pen. Dennis could not even smell what should have been the hog's last smells. He wondered if the hog would haunt this place and decided it probably wanted to be as far away as possible.

The rising sun broke through the grime on the window, bathing them in streaks of mold and yuk. From the cold, Dennis could not feel his fingers, although his feet had finally reached a level of thawing pain.

"I don't bring my hogs to be butchered and cut up somewhere else. People who do that are just too lazy. They don't know the satisfaction of killing an animal you'll eat later. Damn, I can't wait to get a piece of that animal. When I get some of that ham and sausage turned, I'll get ya'll some of the meat. It ain't nothin' but good," said the farmer.

Dennis thought about never eating anything from a hog again.

From behind some old papers on a top shelf, Farmer Jack Victory pulled out a whiskey bottle. Dennis had hoped for a reward like an old book of wisdom passed down through the farming generations, or at least some chocolate candy.

The farmer took several gulps from the bottle's dark liquid, then gave it to Papa who took a taste. He handed it to Herb, who took a long swallow before handing it to Leroy. He took a swallow and burst into a fit of coughing while looking like he would throw up. Dennis took the bottle before Leroy dropped and broke it and handed it to Farmer Jack Victory without drinking any.

The farmer gave a nod and smile to Dennis and put the bottle back. Dennis thought the nod was a salute for doing a good job. The smile maybe satisfaction that Dennis was more mature than Leroy. The farmer led them toward the farmhouse.

The rising sun blared into their faces. Up ahead, Jack's wife Ruth stood on the porch with a large spatula in her dirty hands.

The dirtiness of his clothes and the smell of hog blood made Dennis realize they had been working for hours. He felt rugged, big, and demanding. At that moment, he could fall asleep any-where.

"Got 'em up for a good breakfast, Wife. You ready for 'em?"

"Get your ass in here, Husband. The whole of ya'll. I ain't got all day to mess in the kitchen."

They walked into a small kitchen with knotty pine walls. Fatty smoke seemed to ooze out of everything and made the cramped, heavy air delicious enough to eat. Dennis thought he understood hunger for the first time as a wobbling dizziness took him to a back chair at the round kitchen table. The farmer sat on one side of him with Papa on the other.

They feasted on whatever Ruth put in front of them. Dennis did not care that the sausage probably came from a previously butchered hog or that the whole of the meal came from the iron skillet burned black with a history of lard. The runny eggs, white bread toast, and jar of strawberry jelly hit his stomach and gave him a fading buzz of sweet and fat. He felt his life span shorten. Only the black coffee, strong enough to walk into his mouth, kept him awake.

Everyone except Dennis talked about how great a job they did butchering the hog. When they moved on to talking about sports, Farmer Jack Victory leaned toward Dennis, almost in his face.

"I'm tired of farming," he said.

It was in a deep whisper only Dennis heard. The others were too busy eating and talking.

The farmer continued. "I used to enjoy farming. At the end of a long day, I felt like I'd done something useful in the world. But I'm getting tired of it all. This is not the life I dreamed about. I need to get out, yet I'm trapped. Don't you ever get trapped like me." The farmer leaned back as if he had said nothing and joined the men with their sports talk.

Dennis wasn't worried about being trapped. He was worried about what the hog butchering had done to his psyche. At least the farmer's words and the coffee kept Dennis awake.

What did Farmer Jack Victory mean? Dennis wondered this as he soon felt the fried fat slip across his face. Everything became a blur of memories he hoped to forget.

On the drive home, Dennis had to ask Papa, "Where and when did you learn to cut up a hog?"

"I was about your age when my father took me to a hog killing, just like this one. He wanted me to have that experience, and I went with him every year until I went to college at eighteen. Now I'm not sure it was the right thing to show you. It was a way of life back then, but not anymore. I could have come by myself."

"It's alright. I'm glad you invited me. At least now I know how to slaughter a hog," said Dennis. "But don't be upset if I never eat hog meat again."

Papa smiled and gave Dennis a thumbs up.

At home, Glenda kept asking Dennis about the hog butchering. He wanted to go to bed, so he began at the killing. By the time he got to the throat cutting, Glenda didn't want to know anymore. Dennis wondered what the farmer did with all that blood.

A few months later, Farmer Jack Victory died suddenly from a heart attack. Dennis figured all those animals he slaughtered finally ganged up on him and exploded his heart.

Ruth sold the farm to developers who called the broken farm with the infested muddy pond a beautiful, tree lined settlement on waterfront. Later that year, all semblance of the farm became trampled by the running of children, barking dogs, and passing cars.

With the money, Ruth traveled to Egypt to see the Pyramids, fell off a camel, and died after breaking her neck. The camel ended up being slaughtered for killing a rich American and its meat sold in the butcher's market. Dennis wondered if camel meat tasted like hog.

Kissing in High School

Dennis got his first kiss by a girl at the start of his sophomore year. He was hurrying to lunch since he only had twenty-five minutes and he ate slow when Carolyn bumped into him in the hallway. She had a slanted smile that seemed wicked and catchy. The bump appeared purposely.

"I already heard you want to kiss every sophomore boy before the school year ends," Dennis said, hoping it was enough for Carolyn to move out of his way. He was hungry.

"I plan to kiss a few girls, too. But I won't say which ones."

"I don't care. Why don't you leave me out of your contest?" Dennis didn't want his first kiss to be with Carolyn.

Yet, she had that smile, deep brown eyes, and a cool dark complexion. Her short, curly black hair made her look nothing like his sisters. When Carolyn walked away, glancing back at Dennis with the whites of her eyes showing, he wanted to know more about her contest. At least, that was his excuse for following her.

They ended up under the stairs leading to the gym. Dennis worried about spiders living in the dim lighting as he faced Carolyn. Smelling her musky perfume, he thought that maybe having his first kiss by a professional kisser might give him practice for his next kiss.

"Don't worry, I use mouthwash every morning," Carolyn said, smiling mischievously.

Dennis thought he should leave, but he didn't want to. He let Carolyn wrap her arm around his neck and pull his head down.

He felt he was growing an inch a day and Carolyn seemed to have stopped growing not long after she was born. Focusing on keeping from falling on top of her, Dennis found himself drowning in wet lips with a minty taste.

He wasn't sure what he was expecting. He tried to keep his mouth closed and not swallow her spit. Or her tongue she tried to force into his mouth. Before he knew it, Carolyn stepped away from him.

"That was a good first kiss. But you need more practice," she said with the same mischievous smile. "Thank you for the kiss and any regrets you may have later."

Carolyn trotted away, leaving Dennis standing under the cobwebs in the corner of the stairwell. He spied a leggy spider staring back at him as if saying, "You fool."

The next morning on Thursday, he spied Carolyn leading another boy behind the same set of stairs. She saw Dennis and gave him a wink. He never had anyone wink at him before.

Later that day and the next day, Dennis tried to talk to Carolyn between classes. Yet, she was always in a hurry and her infectious smile became annoying. The more he thought about their kiss, the more aggravated he became that he let it happen.

On Friday afternoon between classes, he confronted her in the school's main hallway. Dennis said, "You need to stop this contest. It's not fair to people."

Almost in tears, she said, "I'm sorry. I shouldn't have taken advantage of you like that."

"You don't even talk to me. And smiling doesn't count. And I don't like my first kiss being part of a contest." Dennis was getting angry.

"Alright, I get it. So that you know, you were my last kiss for that contest and maybe forever. Well, maybe not forever, but at least for a long time. I didn't kiss that boy you saw me with."

"I saw you take him to the stairs."

Carolyn hesitated before stepping a little closer to Dennis. He leaned down to hear her whisper, "There wasn't a contest. I made it all up. I kissed two boys and two girls last year. You were the only one I kissed this year. When I was behind those stairs with that other boy, his hands were all over me and I got scared. I ran away. I'm sorry."

Dennis wasn't sure he should believe her. Carolyn stepped away without her smile and stared at her hands. He was very confused. Why did she kiss him? Did she like him? He wasn't sure he liked anyone, including his sisters.

"Out of my five kisses, I liked yours the best." Carolyn looked up at Dennis with a less infectious smile. More like her true self. "It was the most genuine."

Dennis thought a moment before saying, "What does this mean?"

"It means you and I can be friends, but nothing else." she said. Carolyn stood on her tiptoes, pulled Dennis down toward her, and gave him a brief kiss on his left cheek.

As she walked away, Dennis never thought his first friend would be a girl. Living with sisters and trying to understand them, maybe this would be a good friendship, he thought.

However, before their friendship began, that Monday afternoon Dennis was in the school library waiting to go outside and catch his bus. He was searching for another science fiction or fantasy book to read when Ralph, who was one grade ahead, strode toward him.

He was taller and slimmer than Dennis with a dark, olive complexion like northern Africa, short black curly hair like middle Africa, and eyes like someone from Asia. Dennis wondered why Ralph didn't have girls following him around all the time.

"I want to kiss you," Ralph said as he approached.

"Did Carolyn put you up to this?"

"No, of course not. And I'm not doing any kissing contest. I'd just like to kiss you." Ralph sounded unsure.

"Why me?"

"Alright, Carolyn and I are friends and she told me everything about kissing you. I thought we could give it a try," said Ralph.

"I'm not sure. How would we do this? I guess it would be okay." Dennis never thought about how to kiss a boy. Before Carolyn, he had been unsure how to kiss a girl. Actually, he still wasn't sure how to kiss anyone. He hoped he got better.

Without hesitation, Ralph touched his fingers under Dennis's chin, gently lifted his face up, and kissed Dennis. Ralph's fingers held everything in place with slight tenderness.

The kiss was not wet like Carolyn's, and not dry. It was gradually soft, and Dennis wanted it to last longer. Except Ralph broke away, ending with a soft hug.

"I'm jealous Carolyn gave you your first kiss. But at least I was your first boy kiss," Ralph said. He smiled and gave Dennis a wink before walking away.

Dennis was puzzled about the winking from Carolyn and Ralph. Was this something people who kiss do, like a secret handshake? He tried to wink back and was glad Ralph didn't see. He felt the wink was more like a grimace.

On the bus ride home, Dennis tried to figure out the two kisses. Both were the same, yet a little different. While he enjoyed Ralph's hug, he favored Carolyn's approach and touch. Dennis decided he needed to practice more.

For the rest of the sophomore year, being friends with a girl didn't work out with Dennis. Carolyn had given up on boys, at least for that year, except for Dennis, and she invited him along with her girlfriends. Yet, even growing up with sisters, Dennis struggled to understand girls when they got into a group.

Instead, they talked sometimes between classes, said hello and waved to each other in the hallways, and had lunch together on Tuesdays. Dennis thought that was good enough for a friendship. Being around all those girls Carolyn knew was too much like being around his sisters.

Ralph invited him to join his friends. Yet Ralph had too many friends and Dennis couldn't keep up. But Ralph always reserved Thursday lunch for Dennis, who felt special. At these lunches, he told Dennis how to get ready for the eleventh grade. To Dennis, it was good enough to be called a friendship.

Years later after high school, Carolyn became a stand-in actor with New York City off-Broadway theaters. Her kissing style got the attention of a movie director who brought Carolyn to Los Angeles and promoted her as the "Kissing Queen" in a series of low budget romance movies. She became as talented at kissing women as men.

After two years, Carolyn married the director—a woman—who insisted Carolyn get out of the movies and go back to the theater. In New York City, Carolyn became famous for directing kissing scenes while the director Marge stayed in their Brooklyn home to raise their adopted son.

For Ralph, he dropped out of college after his first year to start a small business redecorating college dorms and other small living spaces. He succeeded enough to move his business to large cities with many colleges.

His signature style became one plainly framed photograph of him in silhouette, kissing men or women who were not in silhouette. This attracted a TV producer and soon Ralph had his own reality show about decorating and designing.

It ran for three seasons until Ralph announced that being famous was annoying. He grew tired of the people he met who were jealous of his fame. He moved to the Canadian island of Newfoundland to get far away from Los Angeles.

Ralph kept in touch with Dennis and told him about living near the Battery with the colorful houses. He invited Dennis to come one day and hike with him the steep paths to the Signal that overlooked the Narrows. Dennis never made it.

At Ladies Lookout, Ralph met Aya, a Japanese woman who used to be a man when living in Tokyo.

They sold photographs of themselves kissing between drinking pineapple crush soda pop and eating spicy molasses cookies called Lassy Mogs. They made enough money to adopt a four-year-old daughter Charlie. However, Ralph had to go back to designing small spaces in big cities, with Aya's help, of course. He had to lose weight.

Dennis's next kissing adventure happened the following year when he was a junior.

Claudia approached him on a cool fall morning as he got off his bus. They had Biology class together and were about to start on a team project.

The teacher made the assignment at the end of yesterday's class. He wanted the students to pick their team members and, as Dennis walked out of Biology class, Claudia poked him in the arm. "Tag, you're with me," she had said.

At the bus stop, she was his height with determined almond brown eyes and true black, chin length hair that flared out in a fit of curls, looking like smiles. She was someone he feared.

As a senior, she managed charity events when he couldn't manage his high school schedule that was prepared for him. Claudia was also one of the most popular kids and did things not to be popular but to help people.

"We were married in another life," she told Dennis as the bus pulled away in a cloud of diesel fumes. "Except I was the husband and you were the wife. I think that's why we're on this team project."

Claudia blocked Dennis from going into the school. He vowed that, after getting his license soon, if he couldn't afford a car he would build one.

"While I agree with you on reincarnation, you picked me for the team. Anyway, can't this wait until Biology class this afternoon? I'm going to be late for my first class and I hate to be late for anything. Also, if you're considering reincarnation as our project, I don't think the teacher will accept it. It doesn't sound like biology. Also, did you pick our other team members yet?"

Dennis agreed to let her do the selecting since she had those determined eyes and insisted. Also, he didn't know enough kids to ask. Afterward, he worried she would pick popular kids.

"I'm considering several popular kids. I'll let you know in class," Claudia said. She had a mischievous grin as she darted away.

Dennis thought that too many girls had mischievous grins. He wondered if there was a library book about how to do team projects with popular kids.

Later, before Biology class started, Claudia told Dennis, "I won't torture you anymore. I know too many people on a team will stress you out, so I thought it could be only the two of us. Small teams are more efficient and simpler and the teacher didn't say how many makes a team. Besides, we're both smart enough to do this by ourselves."

"It's great with me," said Dennis.

"Great. We just need to pick a topic and develop a schedule." Claudia waited for Dennis to sit down before slipping to the opposite side of the class to sit with her girlfriends.

Dennis didn't dare go there. Trying to manage a conversation with one girl was hard enough without dealing with a bunch of them. He wished he had paid more attention to his sisters and understood them better. Although he still wouldn't have sat with all those girls.

After class, Dennis found a chance to talk to Claudia away from her friends when she stayed behind.

"Did you pick a topic?" Claudia had her hands on her hips in a confident Superwoman style.

"I want to do something on quorum sensing in bacteria."

Claudia's hands dropped from her hips as she stared at Dennis. "I knew you were smart, yet that's way-smart. But let's dial it back a bit. That's more like a college project. How 'bout we study how bacteria talk to each other in a general way? We can do a simple experiment so our classmates might understand. Hey, that's a really good project idea you had. Impressive."

Dennis felt his confidence explode. He almost leaned down and gave Claudia a hug right then. Instead, he muttered, "Thanks."

What is going on in my head to want to hug her for complimenting me? He shook his head in disbelief as she walked away to a different class than his.

The biology teacher gave everyone time near the end of class to work on their projects. At the next class, students arranged their chairs in clusters around the lab tables. There was no privacy and a time limit until the next class. Most planned to meet after school.

Before Dennis could offer to meet in the city library, Claudia said, "I'm kinda busy with a charity event coming up. I think we can meet here a few more times and be done. You seem to know a lot about this already, so here's a list of tasks and a schedule. We can compare our progress in class. How does that sound?" Claudia handed Dennis several typed pages.

Dennis nearly cried from disappointment. He wanted to try being friends with Claudia. Based on the schedule, they would easily finish before he had time to do that. "Yeah, this all looks good," he said.

In early December when they finished their project and got the expected A+, Claudia went back to her friends. Dennis had not learned how to make friends that fast. Their lives together seemed to be finished, and Dennis wondered if this was what a breakup felt like.

Their kiss happened at a football game.

On a Friday night, Dennis decided to go where his sisters, home from wherever and for whatever, were not. Papa dropped his son off at the last home football game of the season.

Dennis had no interest in the game. He went when he found out Claudia would be there with the band. She played alto sax that not even the boys attempted. Dennis forever liked the alto sax.

At half time, he seemed to be the only one watching the band playing and marching on the field. He thought they were the best part of the evening. During the game, players ran into each other as often as possible in order to get away from each other. There was no logic.

At half time, the band became a synchronized dance of various shapes parading around the field, which was good since their playing was barely tolerable. Except for Claudia, of course. From the field, she waved to Dennis as he sat in the bleachers. He waved back and was impressed she could keep playing and march while waving to him, or noticing him.

When the band came off the field and before the players came back on, Claudia ran to the bleachers where Dennis sat. With no one else nearby, she leaned over and wrapped her small hands around his chin.

For the slightest of moments, she held his face suspended between her small hands. He smelled the sweetness of her sweat and the warmth from her face as it all caressed his flushed cheeks.

Gently, Claudia relaxed her eyes closed and Dennis closed his as he felt her soft lips flow across his. Dennis went spinning off the planet.

An eternity passed until, like a gentle breeze, her face floated away from him. He opened his eyes to her slight, delicious smile. Without saying anything, Claudia disappeared among the noise and lights of returning football players and spectators.

Until he met the woman he would love for the rest of his life, this continued to be the kiss he wished did not end.

The next day on Saturday, Dennis went to Claudia's charity event at the fairgrounds. She flowed among the crowds, keeping them moving and smiling. All Dennis could manage from her was a happy wave.

On Monday, they met in the school library. Dennis planned to get his driving license that week, so his bus riding would soon end. Although, he would miss his library time. Claudia found him after looking all over the library. He watched her look.

"I believe in reincarnation." Claudia sat at the table next to him.

"I gathered that from before. So do I. Edgar Cayce's books are two aisles over." Dennis pointed in that direction, getting nervous that Claudia would kiss him again. He wanted.to be better prepared.

"Then you'll understand. We're on different paths in this lifetime. Don't worry, we'll get together in a later life." Claudia had that smile.

"What's wrong with this lifetime?"

"More realistically, I'm not dating anyone until I get into college. I want a clear start in my life. Just so you know, my kisses in high school have been reserved for a chosen few. And you were one of the best."

Dennis thought about how much more confident he felt after kissing Claudia. Carolyn and Ralph seemed to be more like practice.

For the rest of the school year, Claudia met him in the morning at the bus stop and they walked to his first class. She was always happy about mundane things that Dennis thought were the most interesting things on earth. Papa had promised him a car to drive to school, but Dennis refused so he could ride the bus and walk with Claudia.

During school, she disappeared among the student population and class schedules. After school, she had band explorations and even more grand charity successes. When she graduated college after three years, she married a short man from India.

They moved to Nigeria where she used quorum sensing to help the people grow crops on their barren land. The cell-to-cell communication in bacteria improved the land so the soil could change from barren to nutrient rich. Except, the only crop they grew was cannabis. Everyone was happy. Even the bacteria.

Claudia was not. Later, she married the next person to kiss Dennis.

Before his next kiss, there was Leela. Starting his senior year, Dennis met her for the first time in English Literature. As he sat in his usual middle of the classroom desk, she slipped into a back desk, followed by five of her friends.

Leela wore a black pantsuit with her thick auburn hair dripping toward her hips. She had blue eyes, purple eyeshadow, and a square pale face. Dennis thought he could spend his life and his next life with her.

"I want nothing to do with you. You're not in my tribe," Leela told Dennis when he introduced himself on their third day of class. It took time for him to get his courage up.

Leela spun around to join her equally dark clothed girlfriends, two of which were probably boys. Dennis had a hard time telling with everyone dressed the same.

With Leela not wanting anything to do with him, Dennis continued to steal stares at her from across the classroom. The next week, he talked to Leela's collection of friends.

He discovered they were into the fantasy that Leela was a vampiress. The more he learned about them, the more he wanted to join. Until later that week when they demanded he get a nose ring as proof of his devotion to their group.

"Paying a stranger to push a needle through my nose and clamping a metal ring there will never happen," Dennis told two of the dark ones, as they liked to be called. Leela hadn't given them their dark name yet.

"You don't get it. You have to become like one of us before you get the chance to kiss Leela," said either a girl or boy. He was never sure.

Dennis quickly got over Leela and her dark friends. He had been getting tired anyway of their negativity and darkness and he was afraid Leela would kill and eat him. Plus, the black clothing would have made him stand out wherever he went in school.

In the end, Dennis felt like he owed Leela something. She had saved him from future obsessions and cults. Also, he was glad he didn't have to figure out how to maneuver around her lip rings for a kiss.

In January of Dennis's last semester of high school, he was all right not having any best friend. He was fine hanging out after school or on weekends with groups of his fellow high schoolers at ball games or festivals and the occasional movie. There was no commitment to hang out after the event, although Dennis would have liked sometimes to be invited along.

Other times he was all right with it. He could only take so much of the high school dramas and worry many felt about their future after high school. Dennis had enough worry on his own with what he would do when he graduated.

He was glad his sisters supported his decision not to have a best friend or a girlfriend or a boyfriend or go to the prom. Apparently, they had a bad time in their senior year of high school and wanted him to avoid social scarring.

Glenda had the strongest feelings against her brother having romances in his senior year. He was growing more agreeable with her way of thinking.

"Don't worry about a relationship until you're out of high school and people are more mature," Glenda told Dennis on a Sunday afternoon before she drove back to college.

After listening to his sisters, he wondered how much more mature college people were than high school. Glenda seemed to be home more than at college.

He worried about her. She was about to finish college and had yet to find romance, maybe her only goal to attending college. Her haphazard life continued to be chaotic in her attempts to find love. Dennis decided he needed practice at getting friends and not rely on learning from Glenda.

On the first Friday morning in February and before classes started, a high school senior paraded around the main atrium in a Teenage Mutant Ninja Turtle outfit. His wild curly black hair standing all over his head easily identified him as the senior. No one seemed to know his name.

As students laughed at him and made jokes, Dennis walked up to the guy, stopping his parade. Dennis ignored the chorus of complaints from other students and waited for the guy to say something. The kid stood there waiting for Dennis to say something.

"Which one of the Turtles are you?" Dennis did not know who the kid was.

"I'm Donatello," he said.

"Why did you pick that turtle?" Actually, Dennis didn't know anything about the Turtles.

"He's a scientist and mathematician, never loses his temper, and is calm and friendly. These are all the things I want to be one day. Also, I like turtles."

"People are laughing at you."

"I'm glad. People will think there's something wrong with me and stay away from me. I don't want friends. I had them and they were too much trouble to keep happy."

"What's your name?" Dennis liked the purple mask.

"Hamilton. You can call me Ham, but not Pork."

Dennis thought Ham could be his first best friend. "That costume looks expensive."

"I made some of it. The rest I bought used online and made repairs. This is my first time wearing it out." Ham spun in a circle so Dennis could see the costume at all angles.

Dennis noticed Ham leaning on a long pole. "What's that?"

"It's called a Bo Staff. But I can't call it that because the high school authorities would consider it a weapon. So I call it Stick."

Dennis hoped Ham was normal enough not to hit him with Stick. It looked hard.

"You play video games?" Ham used Stick more like a crutch.

"Not much. Too many flashes and fast movements bother me. I have fun reading books."

"Good, that's how I am. Even if I play for a short time, I get sick. We're not going to be friends, but I see where this is going."

"Where's what going?" Dennis wondered if this was how friendships began. Someone had to dress up in a funny costume.

"I'm not sure. But this will be my look on Friday mornings, so it'll be easy to find me. Just follow the taunting and laughter." Ham gave Dennis a wide smile as the buzzer rang for classes.

The only time they talked was on Friday mornings when Ham wore his costume. During the week when he did not wear the costume, they had no classes together and Ham moved fast in the hallways to avoid anyone asking him about his costume. On Fridays, the costume kept him from moving too fast, so Dennis could catch up.

The third Friday in February and standing in the atrium before classes, Dennis let Ham monopolize the conversation about his Teenage Mutant Ninja Turtles.

By the first Friday of March, Ham and his outfit were getting boring to the student population. Also, Dennis was still trying to get Ham to talk about something other than how Donatello almost died. On the second Friday in March, Ham tried to ignore Dennis.

"What's wrong?" Dennis wondered if they were becoming friends that Ham didn't want. Dennis didn't want them to be friends like this, either.

In his purple eye mask, he turned toward Dennis. His dark curly hair bounced around like a halo, as he said, "I don't want to talk with you anymore."

"Why?" Dennis was a little glad. If it was a friendship. Dennis didn't know that much about the Teenage Mutant Ninja Turtle story to talk about it all the time.

"It's about wearing this costume on Fridays."

"I thought you wore it on Fridays because it was the end of the school week." Dennis was catching on that he should have asked.

"You asked one time why I chose Donatello and I said he was my favorite Turtle. That was partly true. It was because Donatello survived an attack and lived. Unlike my dad who didn't. He died on the last Friday in January from a heart attack. I wear the costume in my grief. With only a mother already looking to marry someone else, I'm half an orphan."

The fragility in Ham's personality caught Dennis by surprise.

The bell rang for classes, and Ham stepped closer to Dennis, who kept an eye on Stick. He was never sure what Ham was thinking. That was the reason Dennis was unprepared when Ham gave Dennis a brief, slippery, wet kiss.

The only thing touching was their lips. They stood in the crowded hallway with kids running back and forth and Dennis not caring. He liked that Ham was sharing his feelings and his saliva. Dennis thought maybe this could make them friends, after all.

He reached out to Ham for a hug, like Ralph had done. Except, Ham pulled away and waddled in his bulky outfit toward his class without saying anything more.

That afternoon, the school held a pep rally in the auditorium for the basketball team. Dennis went because he was on the school paper and needed to write about the rally. There he spied Ham on the basketball court in his Turtle outfit and surrounded by the cheerleading squad. He seemed to have found people who liked his costume without knowing the real him or try to be friends.

The next Friday, Ham did not wear his suit. It was harder for Dennis to catch up to him.

"I'm done with my mourning. It's time to move on. I'm going to be the basketball team mascot with my turtle costume," Ham said.

"The school mascot is a dog. Are you dressing up as a dog?" Dennis tried to figure things out. If they were in a friendship, it was confusing. He liked the Turtle outfit better than the dog mascot outfit he saw other kids people wearing.

"I realize what my dad wanted me to be. He was a chemical engineer." Ham said.

"You're going to be a chemical engineer?" Dennis was not sure what a person in that career did.

"Oh, no. I'm not good at math. I'm going to write comic books. He became a chemical engineer to have a career, but he always wanted to be a stand-up comedian. I'm no good in front of people, but I like to draw."

Dennis followed Ham's logic and rationale a little. Before he could ask how a turtle outfit could be mistaken for the dog mascot, Ham walked away. He was faster without the turtle outfit.

They still met every Friday morning in the atrium before classes. Ham didn't wear his turtle outfit, but he gave Dennis some of his drawings. They were good, although they had too many turtles in them.

After high school, Hamilton took his college money and published a series of comic book stories about three turtles who saved Los Angeles from sea serpents. After a year, he sold the film rights to a Japanese media company and made enough money to buy a minor beach house along North Carolina's Crystal Coast.

He set up a small non-profit to save sea turtles along east coast beaches worldwide. This included the Akassa coast in Southern Nigeria, near where Claudia lived.

She read about the non-profit and had tolerated enough of her husband and his pot smoking friends. She went to help Ham save sea turtles. A few months after Claudia left, the cannabis farm died and her ex disappeared back to India when the money ran out.

A year later, Ham and Claudia married and turned the former farm in Nigeria into a sanctuary for sea turtles along the coast of west Africa. The logo for the nonprofit was Ham in his Donatello suit and Claudia in her Teenage Mutant Ninja Turtle Venus de Milo, or Venus, suit. Everybody was happy, including the turtles.

In his last weeks of high school, Dennis looked back at his kissing experiences and realized they weren't genuine kisses. They were experiences in style and stress, but mostly experimental in form.

He figured Carolyn needed a goal to feel strong, Ralph wanted acceptance to be who he was born as, Claudia used reincarnation to think of herself as someone other than herself, and Hamilton struggled with grief in a way only he could understand.

At his high school graduation, Dennis's sisters surrounded him with kisses. They were better than the kisses he experienced his entire life. Plus, his sisters added a hug as if they never thought he'd make it to this point in his life.

Dennis was glad he made it so he could have their kisses and hugs. Even Mother and Papa gave Dennis a hug. Dennis thought his parents were mostly happy that all their children had graduated high school. Surely things would get easier with their children, including Dennis.

The Effects of Graduating High School

In high school, Dennis listened to his sisters talk about their university experiences. Which is why he decided to stay home and attend community college.

While part of his decision to stay home was to take care of Mary, Dennis knew the social life at a university would have strangled him with stress. He was already worried people would expect him to act like an adult. He stopped worrying that summer before college when Glenda announced to the family she was pregnant.

She had to tell everyone since she was already showing. Before Dennis bought his college books, Glenda married the father, Leroy, from hog killing days.

Dennis regretted not introducing Glenda to someone he knew. He just didn't know anyone.

The wedding, that Mother called a non-wedding, occurred in front of a magistrate who was also responsible for issuing criminal warrants. The reception was in a rented room of the fire station and ended when the alarms and sirens went off. Someone's outdoor grill had caught fire.

The couple moved into an old apartment building where Glenda spent almost no time in. She stayed at the farmhouse when Dennis was home from classes. She was also there when he wasn't home. Basically, she was always there.

"Are you going to stay married to that guy?" Dennis was trying to study in his room one afternoon when Glenda came in. He was in his first semester and she in her second trimester.

"I'm having his child. I need to give it a try," she said, sitting on his bed.

"Sarah and Wendy don't like him," said Dennis.

"Mom and Papa don't like him, either," Glenda said, slumping across his bed.

"I'll try to like him," Dennis said, still feeling guilty for not finding Glenda a husband.

"Thanks," she said, curling up and falling asleep. Her snoring kept getting louder and he had a hard time studying.

Barry was born just after Dennis finished his first semester. Two years later when Dennis graduated, it became clear to everyone that Barry took after Glenda and adored his uncle. At least Barry was not like his father, Mother would say often. Papa agreed.

Also after these two years, Glenda came to her senses and divorced Leroy. She had a lot of help from everyone in the family. Leroy helped, too. He moved to Thailand with a woman from China while his parents moved to South Africa.

Dennis worried about Barry without a father. But with Mother and Papa as grandparents, Sarah and Wendy as aunts, and he as the only uncle, Dennis believed there was enough family to help Barry be all right when he grew up. After all, Dennis thought, he seemed okay after growing up with three older sisters.

When Barry got older, Dennis planned to caution him about relationships by telling him two of his college experiences.

College Relationships

During those two years at community college, Dennis found people friendlier if no one tried to be too friendly. These types of friendships suited Dennis, who enjoyed the laid-back atmosphere of the campus. Nothing was too stressful until he met two women, one for each of his college years.

In his first year, Dennis dated Stella, who was getting her nursing degree. They met in English class, which was boring to them since they knew how to read and write. She had long, thick black hair that fell down her back. It seemed to pull her tan face up, so Dennis saw mostly her long nose. With her being as tall as he, this meant looking up her nose a lot.

Stella saw the 1951 movie *A Streetcar Named Desire* so many times that she tried being Stella Kowalski from the movie. Dennis hated the movie and, after a few dates, worried about someone training to be a nurse who wanted to be a seriously flawed, fictional character.

The only good thing about their developing relationship was that it showed Dennis how much he disliked inflamed women.

This was a term Stella described herself as, and Dennis thought it suited her. A woman on fire with emotional drama that horrified Dennis. Stella planned to move from the just-kissing phase while Dennis had stopped kissing her. That was when Stella discovered she didn't like the smell or look of other people's blood.

Dennis thought she should have discovered this before she passed out in anatomy class when she first saw someone's blood. She was already half way through her nursing degree when Stella stopped trying to be a nurse.

"I'm quitting school and moving to Sydney, Australia," she told Dennis when she was medically cleared to come back. Stella was there only to sign out of her classes.

They were in the lunchroom, surrounded by vending machines, plastic tables, metal chairs, and a crowd of students who brought their own lunches.

"I guess this is goodbye," said Dennis.

"You want to come?"

"No, I'm still getting used to where I grew up. Why Australia?" Dennis was liking this break up. He wouldn't have to do it.

"It's as far away as I can get without trying to learn another language. Through some family friends, I already have a job as a bartender in the expensive part of Sydney. I bet I can make a lot of money." Sheila's enthusiasm and excitement were drawing the attention of nearby students.

"What are you going to do when you mix a Bloody Mary?"

"I hope I don't get hurt when I hit the floor," Sheila said with a giggle as she danced out of the bland, gray-colored lunchroom.

Starting his second year of college and at the end of his third class on statistics, Martha walked with Dennis to the lunchroom.

She had been staring at him in class, making him feel uncomfortable. He walked faster and she walked just as fast. She had long legs.

Dennis sat at one of the plastic tables with his lunch from home. Martha sat across from him, clenching a bottle of water and complaining about the food that she didn't eat. It didn't look like she ever ate.

She was thin thin with thin brown hair and pale pale skin. Dennis wondered if she was a zombie who would eat him. He hoped he wasn't something a zombie found tasty.

Confused by what she wanted, he asked, "Are you struggling with Statistics class, too? Maybe we can share a tutor."

"Forget it. A tutor won't help," Martha said, gulping her bottle of water.

"I don't know. Some of the tutors here seem pretty capable," said Dennis.

"It doesn't matter. Our stats teacher is a miserable man who thinks teaching community college is below him. He wants to fail everyone in retaliation."

"What are we going to do?" Dennis asked.

"Don't worry. A group of us complained to the dean who already heard the teacher trashing the college's reputation. Any tests won't count and we'll all get good grades."

Dennis wondered how he was going to learn statistics if the teacher wasn't teaching it. After eating lunch and listening to Martha gossip about every student she ever met, she followed him to the trash can where he threw away his wrappers.

With the smell of fermenting trash flowing around them, Martha stopped talking. She ran her long, thin tongue over her thin lips, grabbed the front of Dennis's shirt, and pulled him toward her. When she shoved her mouth against his, it felt like he was kissing a plastic table.

After a few seconds, Martha stood back and told Dennis, "I want to have twelve kids before I'm thirty."

Dennis didn't need to know stats to figure out this meant Martha had to conceive her first kid that afternoon. He wiped his mouth, said goodbye, and dropped the class. He would take it next semester when the teacher and Martha were gone.

The Year After Community College

After graduation, college classmates promised to keep up with each other through social media. Dennis felt social media was too impersonal. Everybody in the world could see what they posted. Even private posts were accessible with a little effort.

He tried emailing them, but it wasn't the social media feel they wanted. Soon, his former classmates populated their social media postings with romance and employment in faraway industries. Dennis wanted to compete and share social media stories about Barry. Except Glenda was already doing that.

A year after graduating college, these former classmates Dennis knew in college populated their social media posts with spouses, pets, and houses purchased. Soon after, pregnancies happened with their social life becoming too busy for them to continue posting on social media.

Dennis accepted this transition of his college friends as he adjusted to his first full time job and living in a construction site.

With his business degree, Dennis got a job working remotely for a global company. Among other programs, they restored drinking water and converted landfill waste to energy. He was satisfied working for a company that restored the environment rather than destroying it.

He continued living at home while trying to find an apartment close enough to take care of Mary, his heifer. Papa was considering getting another heifer to keep Mary company, making Dennis jealous. He was content being jealous. It kept him close to Mary and helped him decide to stay home.

After her divorce, Glenda and Barry moved to the farmhouse to save for an apartment prompting Mother and Papa to renovate the house. They reasoned that, with a new life for everyone, the house should have a new life.

Fortunately, Mother and Papa had already added a wide, enclosed back porch. It opened onto a patio, looking out at the field where Papa grew his crops. Dennis remembered when even the weeds wouldn't grow there.

With hammering and sawing echoing from the house, the five of them sat on the back porch, sharing stories about Wendy and Sarah.

Glenda and Dennis called their siblings every Sunday but filtered what they learned before telling their parents. When Wendy and Sarah visited, they didn't filter anything. The renovations left two empty rooms for Sarah and Wendy to live in if they came home for good.

Dennis Finds Something Beyond Kisses

On a Friday afternoon in June and a year into his job, Dennis finished a video call with co-workers in France. In a few months, it would be his first trip to another country. Instead of trying to speak the language, he found it easier to read and write French.

Before he could take off his headset, Glenda pounded on his door. He jerked it open before she banged the door off the hinges.

"Why don't you knock without banging?" Dennis asked.

"Your video call took too long. We have to leave soon," Glenda said.

"Leave where? I need to take Mary for a walk in the field." Dennis sometimes considered her a big dog.

"You're going to be a miserable person if you don't meet other people," she said.

"I meet people all the time. I just got off a video call with five people. Two of them I met for the first time."

"You've never met any of your co-workers in person. You only see them on a computer screen and they may not even be real. They could be some avatar being run by artificial intelligence. I should know."

Glenda managed social media accounts for people who needed them and either disliked social media, didn't want to be bothered, or didn't trust all that internet stuff.

"I thought you had to leave soon. You want me to watch Barry so you can go out with Jeremy and his ponytail?" Dennis always wondered if his co-workers were AI controlled avatars.

"He cut the ponytail and he looks better. Anyway, Mom and Papa are watching Barry 'cause you and I are going out on a double date. I want my son to grow up with a happy uncle and not someone moping around and lonely."

"I've had some dates." Dennis met a few women from a dating app. He wondered if he was using the wrong app. He also pulled out his list of kids' names who sat beside him on the bus in middle school. He didn't remember any of them.

"Those women had drama issues. Maybe you put in the wrong settings. Any of them would have made you miserable and I would have been miserable seeing you miserable," said Glenda.

"Don't worry, I'm not using dating apps anymore." Dennis remembered how miserable he was when Glenda was married to Leroy.

"Good, that's why I found you someone instead," said Glenda.

"I can find someone on my own." Dennis wondered how he was going to do that. The only people he knew were his co-workers, and he only saw them on his computer screen. He wasn't even sure what part of the world they lived in. He also didn't want to mix work with someone he might kiss.

"You don't know anyone except your co-workers and I don't see any of them as available. None of them live anywhere near here," said Glenda.

"I plan on meeting them in a few months when I go to France. Maybe I'll end up being a world traveler like Sarah and Wendy."

"Sarah and Wendy are one mold and you and I are the other. They travel, which is fine, and we stay home, which I think is better." Glenda finished with her signature smile, that annoyed Dennis since he liked it too much.

"So, who did you find?" Dennis was getting nervous dating a friend of Glenda's.

"You know Helen? She runs the bagel café near the commuter train station in town." Glenda came in and plopped down on Dennis's couch.

Getting rid of Glenda was becoming more difficult. Dennis said, "I know about her. I don't like bagels."

"She also has excellent coffee. The four of us are going out to dinner."

"I don't like blind dates. You should have asked me first."

"It's not a blind date. I know Helen and you would know her if you liked bagels. Besides, it'll be awesome for Jeremy and me watching you on a blind date," Glenda giggled and, before she left, she said, "Wear that blue shirt. It looks better on you. We're leaving in half an hour."

She paraded out of Dennis's room before he could refuse either the date or wearing the shirt.

Helen was already seated at a table she reserved in a chain restaurant that didn't need reservations. She had reddish hair tossed over her shoulders, with thick bangs covering her thick black eyebrows. Her hair was the color of Dennis's freckles. He liked her roundish, soft brown face and green eyes.

"I'm always early," Helen said, standing up and shaking Dennis's hand.

She had a firm grip and was an inch taller than Dennis. Since most of his life had been looking up at his taller sisters, he was comfortable with Helen. Except the handshake made him feel as if he was in a business meeting.

"I prefer being early, too," Dennis said.

She had a pleasant unthinness to her body that made Dennis feel comfortable with his unflat tummy. At dinner, Dennis wasn't sure what he ate. He was drawn into Helen's warm voice and quick smile.

He talked about his Grandpapa dying, catching a football once, and running Papa's rototiller. Glenda added highlights from her perspective. Helen had a fun laugh. Mostly Dennis talked about Shelf Life and Mary.

"I liked your life. You should put it in a book," Helen said.

"He wrote about Grandpapa's life and should have put that in a book," said Glenda, grinning.

Jeremy was still giggling about Dennis catching a football.

"I've been talking too much. What about you?" It was the first time he felt this comfortable with someone.

"I grew up as an only child. My mom had affairs with other men until my dad left her. Fortunately, he took me along. We helped my dad's aunt and uncle run their deli, which is where I learned the restaurant business."

Dennis listened to Helen's strong mellow voice as she told stories about the deli and eventually getting back with her mother. At the end of their meal, they barely noticed Glenda and Jeremy had left.

Apparently, the food was not that great. A year later on their first anniversary, Helen suggested they celebrate somewhere else.

During that first year, Dennis never made it to France. He quit his job to help expand Helen's bagel café to the next commuter train station. Morning commuters didn't give themselves time to eat breakfast at home, but had time to stop at Helen's bagel cafés before getting on the commuter train. A third location was in the planning stage.

Dennis never got used to liking bagels, but Helen did make the best coffee. He hoped one day she would tell him the secret recipe.

During that first year, Dennis and Helen helped Glenda and Jeremy move into one of the new apartment buildings. Right after their one-year anniversary, Helen and Dennis moved into an apartment in the same building. But every Saturday evening the four of them came to the farmhouse for dinner to help Mother and Papa adjust to being empty nesters.

They didn't need much help. Their parents rented the rooms out on popular apps. Whenever Dennis was there, he met different people from around the world. It was like being a world traveler. Sometimes the guests joined their dinners. Everyone visited the bagel café during their stay.

At one of the dinners, Mother announced, "I heard some great news from Wendy. She's coming home to stay for a while."

"Is she bringing Amanda?" Glenda asked.

"Yes, they got engaged," said Papa.

In the years after college, Wendy founded and sold a software company that gave her enough income to become a consultant. She told people how much money she made. They hoped to do the same, but she confessed to Glenda and Dennis that these people had no chance after spending their money on consultants like herself. While living in California, Wendy's long red hair attracted Amanda.

Everyone enjoyed Amanda, who looked like her Ethiopian father and Swedish mother with a dark complexion and blond hair. She was a social media sensation who captured the advertising money of companies who had too much money. She advised them to give her more money, which they did.

Over the next few months, Wendy and Amanda traveled to places they saw in their favorite black-and-white movies. When they went to Casablanca, they stayed for three months. It was from their favorite movie.

While there, they adopted five-year-old Latif, who was a very happy boy without hope of surviving to his sixth year. Latif was the reason Wendy and Amanda came home. They wanted to give their adopted son a better life.

Wendy bought the house she grew up in. In four months, she and Amanda had renovated it to look not like it was when Wendy lived there.

They lived in the new addition built to their tastes. The upstairs of the original house became offices, along with an online yoga and meditation studio. Wendy thought Grandpapa's spirit had come back and was giving off good vibes. It was a good selling point toward online video subscribers.

Dennis rebuilt the treehouse and put up a sign that only Barry and Latif were allowed. It was a big sign. Before school started, Latif learned most of his English from Barry as they sat in the treehouse.

"Latif is my best cousin," Barry told everyone as a means of introduction.

"What's a cousin?" Latif laughed at his own joke. Barry laughed, too, although he heard it before.

Everyone was content enough, except there was a lot of worry for Sarah.

After college, tall and thin Sarah learned to walk with sexual confidence. In a few years, she became the top executive in a consulting firm that provided expensive advice to federal government executives who couldn't write a complete sentence.

She traveled the world and had numerous affairs "for adventure," as she would tell Glenda and Dennis. Sarah never stayed long enough with anyone to have children, but she had lots of scandal.

Glenda and Dennis called her almost every Sunday evening and, as usual, filtered what they told their parents. Such as Sarah's explanation about how she liked to tease and lure, bait and release, with men and women.

Sarah admitted to Glenda and Dennis how she felt guilty her mischievous dramatic antics sometimes ended with emotional pain. Sometimes to another person, sometimes to herself, and always with lots of guilt to go around for everyone. Yet, she couldn't stop.

"She's headed for a big fall," said Glenda after one of their calls.

"Maybe we should visit her. A family rescue plan," Dennis said.

"Nope, won't work," Wendy said when they told her later. "Right now she's talking to you and it would ruin that. Also, she wouldn't listen to you, anyway. I know how Sarah is and she'll get there."

A few weeks later on a Sunday afternoon in late fall, the family gathered on the patio as Papa had an adventure with his new grill. It had been an abundant year for crops, meaning their meal would be mostly vegetables, which excited everyone.

Dennis sat with his sweet tea, watching Wendy and Amanda kick a soccer ball with Latif and Barry. Helen and Mother joined them as Jeremy talked sports with Papa. Glenda sat with Dennis.

From the barn, Mary's mooing told Dennis she needed to be let out into the fenced in field. Papa had rescued from slaughter another heifer for Mary to share life with, and the two became inseparable.

Dennis got over his jealousy since both heifers seemed to appreciate him walking them around. Although they went where they wanted. Mostly they walked Dennis.

Glenda came with Dennis to let the two heifers meander in a section of the field. As Glenda stepped around heifer poop, she said, "Sarah's coming. I got a text from her a few minutes ago. She'll be here soon."

"Is she bringing anybody?"

"No, she has an announcement to make. We'll see when she gets here. I just hope she's straightened herself out."

Fifteen minutes later, everyone turned to see Sarah drive up in an off-white Land Cruiser.

"I thought you only drove Beamers," said Glenda, approaching the Cruiser with everyone close behind.

"I needed a change to include what I drove," she said, emerging in style from the vehicle. She wore the latest long cotton dress in green camouflage with dark blue sandals. Her bobbed dark hair danced around her face.

Before she could say anything more, everyone's hugs flowed around her. Barry and Latif first.

Before Barry and Latif started the hugging again, Sarah said, "Let me tell everyone my announcement. I cashed out."

"What does that mean?" Papa was letting some of his vegetables burn.

"What are you talking about?" Mother asked, stepping in front of everyone.

"I quit my job and left everything behind. With my money, I bought a company near the mountains that flies hot air balloons. And also a mountain top with a small house. I'm headed there now."

Before anyone else could speak, Mother provided everyone with a frown. "What caused all this sudden change in your life? Tell me what happened."

Sarah leaned back against her Land Cruiser, crossed her arms in front of her, and gave a deep, relaxing sigh. As if letting go of her past was final. "I got pregnant."

"You're having a baby?" Glenda jumped in front of Mother.

"No, I miscarried right after I found out. It all happened so quickly a few weeks ago. It made me realize I unhappy I was with my life."

"Why didn't you call me?" Mother gave Sarah a light hug.

"I'm your papa. You should have told us."

"Hold on, everyone," said Sarah. "I was going to tell everyone, but losing the baby crushed me. It also made me realize the job wasn't who I was. I got sucked into a life that was not real. So I quit everything to change everything."

"I'm glad. You had Glenda worried," Dennis said.

"Yeah, Dennis wanted to rescue you," said Glenda.

"Talking with Wendy and seeing how happy she was with Amanda and Latif was a great motivator," said Sarah.

"I was going down that same place until I met Amanda," said Wendy.

"So, what now?" Mother asked, as Papa went rushing back to save his vegetables.

Sarah waited a few moments until Papa came back. "After I quit, the stress just blew away. I didn't burn bridges and tell everyone off, although I would have liked to. I just said goodbye. I've been feeling better ever since. Now, let's eat before Papa's food is burned."

On the way to the patio, Dennis scooted close to his sister. "Why hot air balloons?"

"They're colorful and fun looking. Ever since I saw Grandpapa dead, I've been obsessed with bright colors. It's something he always enjoyed. And the mountain top is as far away from my job as possible. Besides, riding a hot air balloon would be something you'd like," Sarah said as she wrapped an arm around her brother's shoulder. She was still taller than him.

On the back porch, Dennis sat next to Sarah and listened to her tell everyone stories about her life before the miscarriage. Some were funny, too many sad, and others desperate. Papa's grilled vegetables made everything better.

Later in the evening at home, Dennis and Helen were glad they had bagels and coffee in their lives. And of course, each other, they said.

Sarah stayed the night at the farmhouse and the next morning had breakfast at Helen's bagel café before leaving for the mountains. Her mountain top house was only a few hours away.

It took the winter months for Sarah to organize her balloon company. Everyone took turns helping. In early spring, she launched her first balloon rides and announced to the family her engagement to Joe, who supervised the balloon launches.

Joe was taller than everyone and he called his Argentina brothers, sisters, and parents once a week. He also dreamed of being the first person to land on the dark side of the moon. Dennis wanted to go along. Maybe not in a balloon.

The quick engagement surprised no one in the family. Sarah had brought Joe to the farmhouse for Saturday dinners several times. They got along so well that Dennis confided to Helen they must have been married in a previous life. She agreed.

Joe wanted to only handle the launches and Sarah wanted only to manage the business. This kept them away from each other as they worked together. A relationship Dennis thought was like his and Helen's that worked.

One Sunday afternoon, Sarah and Joe came to Helen's original bagel café. She now had three. Sarah wanted some tips from Helen about expanding her balloon business. When they left, Dennis helped Helen prep for the morning. He mentioned he was worried about Sarah and Joe, since they both had strong ambitions.

"Everyone has ambitions," said Helen. "Even you."

"My only ambition is for us to be happy."

"I like the 'us'," Helen said, smiling.

By that fall, Sarah's entrepreneurship expanded the balloon business to several nearby towns. The following spring on a morning meant for balloon rides, she and her crew organized the launching of every balloon and many guest balloons.

The mountain skies were covered in bright colors. That evening before the Smith family and their extended family got ready to go home, Sarah and Joe announced they were pregnant with twins.

A few days later, Glenda and Jeremy got engaged. A few days after that, Dennis brought Helen up to the treehouse. He first asked Barry and Latif for permission.

Dennis wondered how many generations would continue to use it. He hoped a lot. Nestled in the massive arms of the old oak, Helen was ready with her "yes."

Under a clear blue, early morning sky in September, Sarah's mountain top became a place of one wedding. She and Joe, Glenda and Jeremy, Wendy and Amanda, and Dennis and Helen. The mountain was filled with people in colorful clothes that Sarah required for admission to match the balloons that were later launched.

A month later, the newspapers recorded the highest number of marriage proposals from attendees of the biggest wedding on the mountain.

Dennis believed in happy endings. He was happy with this ending.

About the Author

Thank you for reading *A Boy's Life*. I hope you enjoyed my book.

I grew up on a dairy farm in Spotsylvania, Virginia and ended up commuting to the Pentagon from south Stafford County, Virginia for several decades.

To keep my sanity, I wrote short stories with more than two dozen magazines and journals publishing them. I escaped the long commute and politics and moved to New Bern, North Carolina (a place I had never been to before). Here, along with volunteer work, I write novels and belong to writing groups.

My website is https://stanleybtrice.com/

9 780990 926573